Into The Laughing Gas World

Stories by

Rin Kelly

atmosphere press

Praise for Rin Kelly's Writing

"Rin wrote about trauma, about the basic dehumanization of being alive in late capitalism, about mass tragedy and about absurd speculative futures that are just around the corner or happening right now. She wrote stories of futuristic collapse and possibility, as her lens moved between dystopian and utopian possibilities."

Jenny Bitner, *Here is a Game We Could Play*

On her story, "White is for Complacent": "I find her story to be sharp and clever and, most of all, moving in the ways it dramatizes literally the ways in which women's humanity and vulnerability are often subsumed into the dehumanizing world of medicine and/or male objectification."

Professor Jonathan Fink, *Panhandler Magazine*
Western Florida University

"Her writing demonstrated her creative range as a poet, an inventor of characters, a witness to inequalities, a debater of public policy. In one of her stories, published in the *Kenyon Review*, she describes one of her characters who writes letters to the editor: "[She] was just magnificent, all spittle and world-wrecking prose ... you'd hear a kind of happy sorrow in your throat by the end of every letter. By the end, she'd always be calling on us to rise and fight and find our oneness again ..." And here, in these words, is Rin herself. She noticed things. She was a soul voice, a woman working at knowing people and justice, a woman writing with "spittle" and verve and a play of mind and heart."

Carol Samson, *Goose Summer*

Of "Wax Works" (shortlisted for the Pushcart Prize): "... In this wicked little stinger, social satire and speculative fiction converge to burst some techno-utopian bubbles."
The Fabulist

On her story, "Upper Management": "We love this story, its wonderful language and surprising, fresh voice."

Elliot Alpern and Gauraa Shekhar, Editors, *No Contact Magazine*
Columbia University

Of "Seven Million Minutes in Heaven": "... an amazing story of loss, wit, and hope."
Kimberly Bliss, Editor, *Hobart Pulp*

Author's Note

Just as we are forced to contend with a civilization on laughing gas that insists what we're breathing is our own natural air, my characters are born with dignity whose dignity, at birth, is denied.

- Rin Kelly

"Painters—and storytellers, including poets and playwrights and historians, are the justices of the Supreme Court of Good and Evil."

- Kurt Vonnegut, *Bluebeard*

"Love and mercy, that's what you need tonight."

- Brian Wilson, *Love and Mercy*

"In one of the stars...
I shall be laughing..."

- Antoine de Saint-Exupéry, *The Little Prince*

Dedicated to Tony Bar,
who made this all possible

"a kind of happy sorrow"

Contents

NEW FABULISM/SLIPSTREAM

5   Wax Works

8   Kahlo

12   The Best-Known Unknown People Who Maybe Drew Breath Upon the Planet

16   Sorry Scenes in the Bang-Whimper District

19   Sheep *Baah Baah Baah*

24   Tricks in the Cereal Aisle

SPECULATIVE VISIONS

29   Upper Management, or GodCo., LLC

33   Seven Million Minutes in Heaven

37   The Breaking News of Charlie Que

53   Sentient

56   Curated

78   A Letter from Lakeside

MEDITATIONS AND BENEDICTIONS

83   The Bentweed Boys

86   Newborn ~on school shootings

91   Graceland and Greenland and Disneyland

94   Scattered

97   White is for Complacent

105   Kintsugi ~Broken Things

New Fabulism/ Slipstream

"... they'd melt right down
the minute they might become self-aware."

Wax Works

No fewer than three doctors had told Icarus not to get too close to the microwave, but Icarus went ahead and got too close: we came home to find him melted all over the floor. He'd oozed all over the machine itself, down the kitchen counters, into the grooves between the tiles, and dripped all the way to where the kitchen meets the living room. That's where he got himself all gunked up in the carpet, and instead of sitting down for the popcorn—microwave popcorn, there goes that—and watching movies, we had to call Dr. Mark's emergency line and have him come over with the wet vacuum to get the damn kid out of the carpet and into St. Mary's for emergency surgery.

He's a good kid, and it's my fault in a way because I wanted a boy after all these girls, and his dad was about the greatest craftsman the world had ever seen. The fancy degrees, the commendations—it was an obvious thing to create a new little man in his image. The passion had gone out of our marriage, and Viagra was too risky, considering the pacemaker, so even if we'd still been in love, it would have been tricky to make a baby. Enter Icarus. The things you can do with wax are phenomenal these days. The things my husband could do, specifically. He had the world's biggest corporations regularly coming to him looking for a new labor force, a pleasant army of workers who wouldn't burp or belch or unionize or die, who wouldn't get their bodies all shot off or shoot up the place. Workers who certainly wouldn't need to be insured, what with the things you can do with vacuums these days. He was the Leonardo da Vinci of his time, really: a man who hated humans and created humans, who was burdened by being such a future-man. In the early days, when we had to use Mexican-type humans to do the manufacturing labor, he just couldn't take having to be around them at all. I once saw him walk the factory floor wiggling his thumbs in the air and then go up to a worker and stick them right in her eyes: "Stop me before I evolve again! Stop me before I evolve again!" Then he just laughed. And really, they weren't using their evolution very well. Not like he did, my famous future-man.

We couldn't replace those workers fast enough—they just could never produce those replacements fast enough. He wanted everything fast, which was another reason the passion ran out early. That man, in bed! Imagine bedding Leonardo, humping the future like that. Usually, he'd roll over and conk right out. Sometimes he'd say "Evolution invented the orgasm" as explanation, which I suppose meant that mine didn't matter, what with science not knowing what it was for. Not for creation, certainly. Not now. Not anymore.

Those framed letters, those commendations! Cargill, Ford, Tyson chicken, Walmart, Exxon, Apple, Taco Bell. With a handshake they'd walk away with 300,000 wax workers that ran on nothing but the mechanical heart we had that patent for. There was no way those creatures would evolve into anything. No, sir. Aim a beam at them—that was another great patent, one that paid for all our bullion investing, his "knocked-up gold"—and they'd melt right down the minute they might become self-aware. Not that that ever happened. Not with the flesh kind, either. But we made good money coming up with patents like that.

There was the one thing, the one glitch: human error. It just couldn't be engineered away. "Do not put a microwave in the break room," he'd tell them again and again. Honda, Tinkertoy: under no circumstances should  you put a single microwave in any break room! The reason they'd always go ahead and do it anyway made sense because until you can replace all your humans, you want them powering up as quick as they can, and they still ran on food—Cargill, the agro giant, was a customer after all. But that was the old way of thinking, before our patents changed the world. I remember one night when he was working on Icarus, cradling that precious little head in his arms. He said to me,

"Cait, the past is full of losers." We had been half men, half beasts, built by chance and stumbling around. But here was the child of the man of the future! A child who would never put a microwave in a break room. But General Electric and Samsung, they couldn't see what my husband had seen—so off he'd go into the night with his vacuum and his tools, off to clean his creations out of the carpets. I told him—I begged him—not to go into those break rooms. "Jesus, Tom, they can get a janitor to do basic retrieval!" But he just couldn't trust his creations to losers. He was a workaholic, that man, and his heart strained beneath his pride. So here we are tonight, just the girls and me and our precious fixed-up Icarus, whispering our precious fixed-up Icarus, whispering our prayers in the ICU.

Kahlo

There was a problem with her heart, and it was an unfortunate but not uncommon event in those days that the health insurance money simply ran out just as they were finishing the operative part of the operation—the part where they'd fixed the part that was broken and had only to tidy up and sew all the bloody bits back in place before heading out for sashimi or movie night or to a fundraiser for the American Heart Association. At the exact moment the money ran out, all that was left was to put the beating, squirming, underwater-alien thing (its valves like seafloor vents, its contents untidy mysteries) back into her chest and wheel her to the big elevator with its extra-wide-gurney considerations for the prone and dying and dead, into a sunny recovery room newly named after someone whose family had been inventing new chemicals for generations.

Back in those days, it was truly believed that there just weren't enough chemicals yet on planet Earth, and humanity was perpetually preoccupied with arranging and rearranging molecules without really caring much about the long-term consequences. When they cared, most of them cared only indirectly, preferring to see the consequences dumped in other counties or countries or handed off to various solemn, scoldy, professional consequence-handlers—non-profit do-gooders desperately doing their goodest with money that often came from the sons of the sons of the original chemical makers in the first place. In those days, the sons of sons of chemical makers, and often their fathers and grandfathers too, liked occasionally to change out of their suits to go talk in tuxedoes in big ballrooms named after oilmen about the human family—each of whom was miserably dependent in some way on the generosity of the chemical makers—then stumble into the little elevators of the upright, hit the penthouses, and fix on oxytocin with various mistresses or maids.

The woman had actually been a maid once—for one of the big

maiding companies of her day—until all that chemical exposure bit through her heart and she couldn't handle scrubbing anymore. So she had been a maid once, but now she was barely anything at all—just the unemployable daughter of the daughter of a maid, coughing and chest-clutching and desperately in need of surgeons to fix her heart so that she could work again. And unless she could work again and work again soon, her insurance would run out completely; some poison-ous-sounding thing called COBRA was picking up the tab, something short-term and shrinking she assumed was for people poisoned by their jobs. It was the COBRA money that must have finally vanished while her chest was open and she was dark in dreamless sleep; it must have been the COBRA, she figured later, that called up the surgical bay that day and called it all off. It was because of the COBRA that she awoke in that sunny recovery room with her heart strapped to the outside of her body by blood-soaked, used-up, barely sticky medical tape. The doctors had repurposed a whole gob of it that had come off a magnificent boob job earlier that afternoon.

"Excuse me, but why did you not put it back in?" asked the wom-an, perhaps too politely, as women were expected to do in those days. (It must be noted here that this is merely the spirit of what the woman said—the language she spoke has unfortunately been lost to history. It was one of those weird, clattery languages anyway, and even back then there was no translator for her at the hospital, not to mention on the insurance company hotline or anywhere in their shimmering tower building with the Diego Rivera mural near the entryway.)

"Bahukhs gaboob tlabooba," they responded, at least according to her memory, though they may actually have been saying "boob" at one point due to the involvement of the magnificent boob job. What-ever it was they were saying, she used her remaining time to sweetly ask again and again why they'd just stuck her heart atop her boob and wrapped the whole thing up with tape. It wasn't her remaining time because what they'd done was about to kill her—they were good doctors, well-meaning doctors, not the least bit unkind, and they had done this many times before. It was simply her remaining time to ask them why.

Soon the first-generation anesthetics and painkillers her COBRA had approved would wear off completely, and after that it would be many years before the woman learned to speak through the strange, chilled pain of wearing one's heart hoisted up by floral wire and ribbons and extension cords and, in the privacy of her own home, the leftover entrails and valves and veins the doctors had given her so that the whole thing would feel organic, less like something done to her and more like something bodies just did. Besides, it was all they could afford.

In those days, when the heart was hurting, it could be very hard to talk.

The woman's sister sat at her bedside, squeezing her hand. They looked so much alike that, looking back on their world with the advantages of ours, it might objectively be considered a blessing that the woman acquired this new heart condition. For the first time, people would be able to tell the twins apart—even their mother had had difficulty with it for several years, back before she acquired a condition of her own.

Vision, much like our 2wenty2wenty mech, was one of the five organic senses of this particular era, and it wasn't uncommon in those days for the loss of one sense to heighten the others. It was only after there had been an accident involving cleaning chemicals and the older woman's eyes—a little splash of  household cleaner to the eyes could lead to heightened hearing—itself a kind of blessing, for in time the mother learned how to listen for the little differences in her daughters' voices.

It would not be long before the woman was no longer able to speak at all, at least for several years, and she used her remaining time to politely ask again and again why they'd simply wrapped up her heart with boob tape. It wasn't that what they'd done would somehow take her voice—it was just that soon the pain would kick in, the first-generation anesthetics her insurance had grudgingly paid for would run out, and, when the heart was hurting, it could be very hard to talk. And later, when she'd learned to speak through the strange, chilled pain of wearing one's heart over to the center from the sleeve, the average person simply looked away, spoke instead to buildings or to halfway areas of air, because it was a natural thing, back when humans still had such organs, to pretend that you weren't essentially made up of such things, guts and spleens and oozing, squelching things that were the ones actually doing the work—and that they'd eventually run out of the energy for working, as all workers back then simply had to do. The average person liked to pretend that he or she didn't have one of those, or guts and spleens and oozing, squelching things that were the ones actually doing all the work. Sometimes people would care— they'd guess correctly that it was because of Life Insurance, LLC, or Life, Incorporated—but when they'd start their rants (these goddamn corporations!), something about it reminded her of her maid days, like with those people she was a means to an end.

It shouldn't have been surprising that so many men used it as a chance to grab an eyeful or cop a feel. Her breasts were slimy with blood, yet the powerful play goes on, and all men, of course, are asked to contribute a verse. "Is that real?" they would ask again and again. It was something they'd long asked of her breasts—now they asked it of her heart. She got the sense that they cared less about the truth as it applied to her than they did about what it meant about what their own hearts might look like and were relieved they hadn't been born a woman. Then they'd stumble into the little elevators of the upright with mistresses or maids, hit the penthouses, fix on oxytocin.

A breast is alien when attached to a heart. A breast isn't meant to circulate blood. A breast isn't meant to give milk, really—that's something that happens sometimes, but it's really beside the point.

So it was not long before, in some room named for some man of molecules in a wing named for a man of money in a hospital named for a chemical maker, the woman awoke to find a woman at her side cradling a whole network of tubes and holding her hand in place of an IV.

The Best-Known Unknown People Who Maybe Drew Breath Upon the Planet

Back when we were all suddenly out of our jobs, I started writing letters to the editor every day. Then it was twice a day, and soon I was writing all day long. There were dozens of me: Amelia Wren, Colin Shaw, Julio something, a street musician named Wando, Jesus Christ—by which I mean that I thought I was Jesus Christ; I wasn't really Jesus Christ. And I wasn't exactly crazy, either, not the brand of crazy you usually see with Jesus Christs or expect from Jesus Christs in the day-to-day. I was more of a guy impersonating Jesus Christ and doing a piss-poor job.

So I was him—I was He—and I was a widow named Marjorie, and I was her nemesis Raymond, and also a Wyatt something-or-other, an agoraphobic crossing guard whose life was a real tragedy that no one, tragically, ever quite recognized. No one but me. I had a lot of love for Wyatt. Had there been a Shakespeare around to notice his nobility, it would have really been something. Were that there was someone around to notice all of our nobilities. Not "our" our—Amelia and Marjorie and Julio and me—but all of us, really.

Raymond had a real bone to pick with the school board, which he thought was taking God out of the schools, as though God had ever really been there to begin with. Marjorie hated Raymond, and they'd have some gorgeous fights in the opinion pages about all manner of things. Fights in the literal opinion pages: I graduated a few of me up from letter writing to submitting op-eds, and then letters would flood in from people loving what I'd had to say, or hating it, or hating me, and while many of those letters were from me, many were also from real people, or from people who claimed to be real people ... who can know? After a while I wasn't sure if a letter was from me or from someone real—but not real necessarily, just from someone who wasn't me. In time there were so many of me I couldn't always tell who was me and who wasn't.

Marjorie was just magnificent, all spittle and world-wrecking prose, so much dignity and clemency that you'd feel a kind of happy sorrow in your throat by the end of every letter. By the end, she'd always be calling on us to rise and fight and find our oneness again ... though not "again," really, because we were never all one. That's a cliché-ish sort of construction Marjorie would never use. It's the kind of thing Raymond would say, now that I think about it—he always wrote his stuff as though there were some idyllic yesterday we all had to resurrect. Marjorie knew that wasn't real. And if God really had been in the schools, the roof of the old schoolhouse that hid her away as a kid would have peeled back and a big sun-stirred pillar of air would've beamed down and pulled old Marjorie above for all to see. She was that big a talent. A lot of people you wouldn't expect to be are. She would have written beautifully about Wyatt the crossing guard, but for reasons I can only guess at—tragic reasons or just the day-to-day—she never did anything with her talent other than writing letters and op-eds. That happens a lot, too.

I don't mean to sound like I was ever against Raymond or looked down on Raymond in any way. He was smart, and he was successful for a while—he ran a chain of car dealerships, I think. So, when gas prices started getting too high and those big trucks he sold weren't popular anymore, everything must have really gone to hell for Raymond. His wife probably got so sad over that that she took one of those big SUVs from the lot, decorated it up the way you see high-school kids do at graduation—Goodbye, Class of ____!—and added some balloons and some tinsel and then killed herself right in that car. With carbon monoxide, the way they do. I sure felt sorry for Raymond then. And his wife—what a sense of humor she had!

So I don't mean to disparage Raymond. He took citizenship very seriously, and he never existed just to make Marjorie look better no matter how often they sparred. It was never meant to be like that at all. Raymond wasn't the writer she was, or the personality, but he did what he could, and for most of us that's its own sort of brilliance. Especially after what happened to his wife. And to his credit, Raymond also was never overbearing in that way that inspired many a letter from me calling Marjorie to account. Bale J. Thornton, North Balen, thought she was everything wrong with America; Polly Someone was especially harsh, though I always suspected Polly was actually Raymond. But in the end, Raymond did mean well in his way. He just believed that the past was a place, and he believed we could all return there.

There were many weeks when every letter published was one of mine, and there were a few when all the letters were mine and about my op-eds and picking bones with other letter-writers who were also me—and those would all run beneath six of my op-eds, too. There were some beautiful people in those pages in those days, not just Marjorie and the crossing guard. Paulo was a real fighter, dogged, all truth, and he worked like hell trying to convince us that the city council should be focusing less on building a luxury housing development on the old plating-factory grounds and more on relocating everybody right away, on reopening the molybdenum mine outside of Cooper and getting us all out and working. I, me, me-me, tended to agree with Paulo-me on every count, though it had been me—it had been I?—who started the movement to bring a luxury development in. I can't remember which one of me that was. Probably Tanya, who literally had no soul.

They never published Jesus' letters or op-eds, which literally made me laugh, because if the real Jesus were to arrive on Earth he surely would be deemed too mad to ever get his message into the papers, especially on the extra-hot topics of housing developments or God in schools, where the competition is tough and editors tend to allow only one type of crazy through. Those are the sorts who show up at every council meeting to rant like maniacs about zoning changes or how a partial nuclear meltdown is no minor thing—the people Marjorie, the inimitable Marjorie, called "pathological citizens" not that long before she died.

I only strayed from the opinion pages a few times, usually just an obituary here and there. Wyatt won third place in a photo contest once, and Wando the street musician took out an engagement announcement with another one of me I can't remember. Marjorie wrote the announcement—and as usual, she went too far. No one in her world was just proud to announce the engagement of so-and-so

from somewhere, someplace, child of someone and someone else entirely, to another so-and-so who'd been born at some particular point
in time. To Marjorie it only mattered that when a pair of somebodies
fall in love, they become "aligned with a great eternal pity that has
always been wiser than God." Then she went off into a big reverie
about how love only has power because it's not survivable, which was
in pretty bad taste in a place where people were dying all the time.

After a while I died too, and it doesn't pain me as much as you'd
think to say that no one mourned me in the opinion pages. I only
wrote in a few times, and I'm not much of a writer myself, so I was
mostly ignored. There was a lot less opposition to Tanya and Raymond after I was gone, though, and that was a pity because, in time,
Tanya became mayor and rallied public opinion around the housing
development. The town never moved, and the mine never did reopen.
Wyatt the crossing guard was just wrecked over that. He would have
been so happy working in that mine.

I'd long had an idea for a story, a story about Marjorie and how
in heaven you meet all the people who had been the greatest poets,
the greatest minds, the greatest dancers who ever lived, and you're
expecting to see Shakespeare or Newton standing there, but it's just
some person. Some Marjorie who ended up hobbled for some reason—
some poor soul assembled in heaven, made sane, shaken continually. I
never really got around to writing the story, which happens a lot, too.
Still, I always had it in mind, but when I got I found out it was an idea
I'd unconsciously stolen from someone else, a story I read long ago.
I think it was by Mark Twain, but I could never find him up here to
verify. That's not to say that Twain went to hell. There is no hell. But
there's no Marjorie here either. Truth be told, it's a lot lonelier than
you'd think.

Sorry Scenes in the Bang-Whimper District

At the intersection of Baker and Poole I died slipping in matchstick rain off the corner into the gutter, head to the grate, and ended up with blue-black stripes all down my face. They had a bitch of a time handling that at the funeral home. At the intersection of Baker and Poole I died in the punishing flash of a thousand-degree heatstroke that wasn't what I'd ever been expecting. I'd been expecting cancer—at some point I'd started expecting it all the time. Sometimes I'd try to make use of it, to tell myself *live, live, life is too short!*, but my mind never wanted to listen to that. Even to the very end it wasn't listening to me, and instead of the life-flash life had told me tends to come at the end, I found myself worried what the other people waiting for the crossing signal would think of me, lying there. What could they have been thinking? Probably about death and then not about death, because you just don't ever want to think about death too long. At the intersection of Baker and Poole a cab whipped around the corner, and I'd just whipped my head in the other direction to look at a girl's ass, had stepped out into the street without doing the one true thing I learned as a child: always look both ways. She was a teenager, the ass. It's no longer worth putting on the old act and saying something like, "It was worth it!" because it wasn't. Honestly? My thoughts went right to my wife. She'd put on a lot of weight after the girls, and what an ass I'd been to think this made me something of a loser in life.

At the intersection of Baker and Poole I had a bright whiff of something pleasantly burning and then was gone. No idea what the hell that was about—I couldn't stick around to find out. I would have liked to have at least known. Did I matter so little? How is this fair? At the intersection of Baker and Poole a pickup hit my bike.

At the intersection of Baker and Poole I was just so sick of epiphanies. At the intersection of Baker and Poole I was dreaming about my impending fame and was so late that morning I'd rushed out of the house without my inhaler. There was a street musician working the corner that day, the young guy with the recorder of all things, playing "Jesu, Joy of Man's Desiring," and I was so quietly proud that I recognized the song. Even though I was wheezing harder than ever before, I wanted to say the name out loud to someone but couldn't find a non-clumsy way to do it, to show how learned I was. At the intersection of Baker and Poole memories kept smacking at me, and suddenly bullets were smacking at me, and I didn't last long enough to learn why.

At the intersection of Baker and Poole isn't it a beautiful day? People were shot right here decades ago, but today is today. At the intersection of Baker and Poole it was like there was a pack of maniac fire ants up my legs and in my head, and I stood up from my cubicle and looked around. I remember seeing a plane crossing the big, blameless blue sky beyond the windows that looked down on Baker and Poole. I'd seen someone die there once—slipped right off the gutter and into the grate. There had been a lot of screaming; I don't know why I didn't scream for help when my turn came. There were halos in my vision. I just watched the plane cross the world. Everything was smoking at the edges—wasn't it beautiful, that sky? Sometimes I just couldn't stand it.

At the intersection of Baker and Poole a plane flew right into our building. It was an accident, a small plane, and I would never admit this to anyone, but part of me was annoyed that it wasn't terrorism that did me in. People just weren't as interested in us. We weren't national news—even locally things moved on pretty quickly—and we weren't symbols of anything, not mourned as anything meaningful, just unlucky souls. Not that many, luckily. Would we have had more attention if there were more of us? I always wanted attention. Not too much, not anything excessive, just enough to feel like the world was there to bear witness. Was that so wrong?

At the intersection of Baker and Poole a bomb went off and everyone came to help me. It was beautiful how people forgot themselves, and because of it, they'll never forget me, I think. At the intersection of Baker and Poole I'm running, and it's morning, and the sun's just breaking golden in that part of the day when it's like you're sharing secrets with the early-hours shopkeepers and delivery drivers who are bringing food and life and things, and maybe sometimes near-death in a sudden swerve, who are bringing bagels. At the intersection of Baker and Poole I want a bagel so much, but I'm not attractive enough just yet, so I keep running, running, and I'm running and running and run over by the bagel truck. I stay conscious for a few days, which everyone thinks is lucky.

At the intersection of Baker and Poole isn't life magnificent? The city is a living thing. There are smudgy streetlights sabotaging the darkness, and looking up at them, into the mist and mystery of it all, you could be in a movie of your own life—it's that kind of night. The universe is peeking in to bear witness, and everything, for a minute, is momentous and clear. At the intersection of Baker and Poole I'm sitting by my window looking down and thinking idly about jumping into the still evening.

At the intersection of Baker and Poole there is green life snaking up out of the pavement cracks and gutters. At the intersection of Baker and Poole we met cute at that little coffee shop and parted at that coffee shop, at the intersection where the cute little coffee shop now stands dead. Life took it, roots twisting up and around and through, vines intersecting and weaving weedy wastelots out of streets and houses and furry long blocks where buildings serve no purpose but to throw shadow shapes against the sky. At the intersection of Baker and Poole a new form emerges.

At the intersection of Baker and Poole there once was an intersection of her and her, her and him, him and him, him and them, them and bumper, cancer, liver, lover, sky, of Baker and Poole, Poole and Sherman, Sherman and Livingston, Livingston and 5th, 5th and Sunset, Sunset and Morningside, Morningside and Waking, Waking and Good Morning, Good Morning and I Love You, I Love You and Embarcadero, Embarcadero and Commerce, Commerce and Home, Home and Kiss, Kiss and Sunset, kidney, climate, comet, sky.

At the intersection of us, you could not save my life.

Sheep *Baah Baah Baah*

In the years before the god famine no one below has ever been told about, in the years when there were many and they were messy and then Upstairs cleaned things up a bit—it was Upstairs, it wasn't the lot of you who brought forth Allah and all of that—there was a mighty argument that rent the whole world, that made the whole world in two.

Some were on the side of a Greek god we'll call "Bill." Others were on the side of a Greek god we'll call "Dan." Using their real names might embarrass somebody because, monotheism be damned, they're still out there with their minor influences causing minor earthquakes and laughing together in some Waffle House somewhere about how scared that family was of the "poltergeist" living in their refrigerator, what a laugh, that sort of thing.

This particular god war started not entirely because of what Bill did or what Dan did but because, even before it happened, some of the gods, Greek or otherwise, were already in the Bill camp and some were already in the Dan camp, just as gods, just as friends, just as groups of supernal beings who had similar powers or origin stories or just generally got along. It wasn't all that different from when some human peon divorces some other human peon and the friends who can't stay magnanimous find themselves picking sides and believing the horrible stories of one over the other. It was actually the lack of difference from that sort of situation that made the whole thing remarkable at all.

Bill had come to Earth as some sort of animal I can't really get into. Let's just say Bill had turned himself into a sheep. Back and forth he would go from the god place and the people place, tricking them with his animal shape, taking their women, playing strange pranks the way gods always used to do. But he did something to anger someone we'd best not mention, and before long, he was no longer able to stop being a sheep. As a sheep, he was suddenly stuck roaming the earth, and just like in some kind of Disney movie, he would be a sheep forever until someone felt a particular, strong affection for him—not deep, true love, just a sort of love one mammal might feel for another that's stronger than pack instinct, stronger than being locked together in the same eventual dance with death at the same time in history, stronger than that kind of get drunk and I-love-you-maa-aan kind of love.

It's hard to explain god-thinking, to explain the love Bill's punishers had in mind. It was a specific lesson he was to be taught—a lesson very much related to the bad thing he had done. Make someone fall for you! In exactly this way! It really did happen that way sometimes. Occasionally fairy tales do get things partly right, and it's possible that the Grimms or whoever else had a hand in putting them on paper had help from some bored god post-monotheistic-diktat or just had that influence without really knowing it. So Bill roamed. And quickly he realized that, while sheeplike, he was still no ordinary sheep. He was an eternal sheep, an immortal sheep, fated to watch flock after flock die and become dust without a single one of them ever loving him because they were sheep and they didn't understand him, because they were sheep and he still smelled like a god to them.

After a few hundred years of this, and entirely out of coincidence, the god "Dan" had a wild hair to play games with the sad little peons. He was one of the bad seeds of his little god-group, and if you know your mythology, that's saying a lot. He was a boundless asshole. So Dan wandered on down from where his family lived—it would be too obvious to say where—and took it upon himself to romance women all over the world and get them pregnant with little god babies. In his human-looking form, he wasn't as stunning as a non-god would expect a god in masquerade to be.

For some reason, he had bouts of cystic acne, which were maybe his mother's doing, as he was her least favorite. He was passably handsome, though, and he smelled of perfume, an unearthly perfume no one had ever smelled and would never smell again. It wafted from him naturally, from his cystic boils. That attracted a lot of women to him. "What is that? Where can I get that?" And then soon, boom, they were in bed. But while Dan was wandering the Earth impregnating women with babies who would then go on to be gods themselves, gods in culture after culture you probably know, gods of all shapes and forms, gods whose mothers Dan had turned, with his ethereal sperm, into various non-human creatures, his mother decided This Ends Now! and made him a plain old human-human behind his back. Not permanently, for he was her son after all—just for a hundred years or so, until he'd grown up enough to come back and properly rule his share of things. Soon the god-babies were just baby-babies born to mothers Dan had found himself not wanting at all, nor they him really, and the heavenly perfume dried up. Dan learned what it was to be human, and alone, and lost, and to cry at night hoping some god somewhere would hear him. He would promise to be good if the gods would cure him of this human disease, oh please, oh please. Did he even believe in them now? In the existence of gods? It might have just been a dream. He would cry and ask the gods why he had been burdened with having so much capacity to feel and think when there was no way to just blink himself away into some other situation where there was no need to meditate on—to marinate in—one's feelings the way he suddenly had to do.

"Being human hurts! I hate this! I hate me!" he would cry into the universe, his back giving out, his erections dimmed to nearly nothing, his mind given to perpetual worry about things from the past that could do nothing more to him now than could the slightest breeze— memories which nonetheless spun and spun and spun in his head as indictments of his being, of his place on Earth, his basic lovability, his worth. He had been created as nothing but worth, so this was an impossible experience.

There was another god from his general god-clan, a god we'll call "Jenny," who had been Dan's lover for a thousand years or so at the time of Dan's departure. Jenny wasn't much bothered by Dan's human partying at the time, as she had been busy among the humans herself for a while, turning back and forth from a man to a woman and back again and back again just to test out various theories about what sorts of ailments different genders ought to suffer. But in her travels, she began finding herself among whole villages of god-babies, powerful little beings or just kids born prodigies or with the most beautiful web-toed feet. And it wasn't that Dan had been "cheating," because polytheism was full of poly-absolutely-everything. It was that he had been making minor deities when he ought to be making major ones with her.

Jenny could hear Dan's cries at night, though usually gods never do. He had begun to believe that a woman he had impregnated, a woman he hadn't loved when he was a god and whom he barely remembered in his human form, a woman he now found haunting his human dreams (dreams were new to him, were making him delirious, making him mad) was the love of his life, had perhaps been his wife, and that something bad he'd done had driven her away. He was mixing up his heavenly something-bads and his earthly something-bads, which weren't all that bad at all compared to destroying villages and inventing smallpox. But now, as a human, Dan felt a kind of heavy, winter-wet coat of regret hanging from him at all times. What had it been, what is it that I did, what is it that's wrong with me? Why am I decaying? Why am I alone? And Jenny thought it would be funny to end his loneliness for a while by making him fall in love with a sheep.

Oh, how they loved! Do not try to imagine it—just trust that it happened, that they loved; they were lovers. And still Dan would cry at night, arms cradling Bill, lonely even then for something more human, something that could return the gentle stroking of curly hair and beat back, for a moment, the death that circled his mind constantly: it's coming! It's coming! It's not fair, it's not fair! If only there were someone to put her arms, his arms, two opposable-thumbed arms, around my waist, to tell me in return that you are loved, Dan Whatever, you are loved like buttercups love the dew, the sun. And Bill yearned for the language to say it, too, this earthly love a god had never experienced before. In all his thousand years, he had never loved like this. They made love until the sun came up, until the sun burned off all the dew.

For a moment, when their love had at last become something approaching the eternity they both had taken for granted for many thousand years, human Dan and sheep Bill began to glow golden and wheels of air drew halos around them, Dan believed this was death defending, Bill believing it was some sort of sheep stroke. And then suddenly there they were, two gods from two god houses, lying there in the hay, two tangled-up, fragrant god bodies. There wasn't even an alcohol-fueled night to explain this behavior away. They had both jumped fully into a filthy, earthly love. And suddenly there was no love between them. There came thunder and cyclones and horrible bouts of syphilis, which is something Dan had invented with Jenny—together, for aeons, they had been the gods of that particular disease. Bill turned the weather upon Dan, upon his friends, and upon his whole house, and pretty soon all was gossip and threats of holy war.

Gods were petty in those days, and this was possibly the pettiest spat of all. Things like this just didn't happen when you were toying around with Earth—it wasn't that there were rules against it; it just didn't happen. Everybody gossiped. Friendships fell apart.

There were stories on this side and stories on the other, none of them true, accusing Dan or Bill—or Jenny, too—of having done things when it was really all just a terrible misunderstanding. The ugliness only increased when everyone ended up punished for the various gods' mistakes with new rules about how much you could fuck with humans, could fuck with sheep. Everyone loved messing with the peons! Ultimately, over the years and following several other events, catastrophic and minor, the Bill-Dan dalliance helped push Upstairs toward a monotheistic system of government. Which left a lot of gods shit out of luck and just wandering around, making little cyclones, killing off the bees. But they say tragedy plus time equals comedy, and when you hear a sheep going *baah*, going *baah-baah-baah*, that's the gods laughing through them, because, in the end, it was all awfully goddamn funny.

Tricks in the Cereal Aisle

The cereal aisle was brightly alive with childhood and death, the adult world looming atop the higher aisles, below—so cynically at toddler height, even now in this era of enlightenment—the sugar-giddy tigers and frogs of youth that would grow someday to Grape-Nuts height and the terror of heart disease. Tricks, for the first time, felt a proud pang of superiority standing there, superior to that whole human world, reading the box-front badges about Omega 3s and vitamins that might, just might, oh God please, prevent human wreckage and decay. He himself would never decay—eternal, he could only become obsolete, but not today. Not today.

Today was joy and redemption, and it didn't shock or rock him to his core to see with his own eyes at last that he had been replaced. That he'd been sacrificed to those same bodily terrors and slain on the altar of the natural that was humanity's new great mirage-god. All the aisle was all natural now, all-natural all-sugar all-real-fake flavoring—and there on the front of the new Trix box was a natural, real rabbit happy to hawk what was suddenly natural about corn-made-fruit-shaped sugar barf.

Okay, it wasn't sugar barf. It was manna from General Mills. He'd spent his entire life trying in something a lot more than quiet desperation to get a bowl of the stuff. Twice the powers had allowed him, in 1976 and 1980, because the children of the world had voted to make it so—those very same children who since 1960 had been snatching his manna back with a "Silly rabbit!" and the invocation of one of those strange human rules as silly as any rabbit and as arbitrary as it was sacredly true.

He picked up the box, shook the box, savored the feel of the box in his hand, and a terror seized him that even today, a girl and boy would blink into existence—Silly rabbit!—and steal it away. Trix were not for him, said the human world, for reasons they themselves had never sought to understand; Trix were only for kids, kids who didn't even buy the stuff for their damn selves. Since the end of Eisenhower, since before Civil Rights, he had been smiling away the pain of knowing just how much of life was a listless lie believed for the sake of believing in something, for believing in a continuity and order and purpose to human life—he had been grinning as his guts churned. But today, contract fulfilled, released from his very purpose in the world, he was free to act on all he had learned from this subjugation. Ha ha, kids: now he had money for the stuff, and no parent, no law, no fussy human world could ever again say, Tricks, this particular joy is not for you.

Did they know his name was Tricks, all the way back to the beginning? Did they know he was his own man, that he wasn't "the Trix Rabbit," that he had a wife and two children who'd been getting by on generic fruit-flavored, sweetened, ground-corn pieces since 1982? "The Trix Rabbit": as though he would call himself after everything life denied him! Who were they, these three-dimensional creatures with their two-dimensional ideas, their limbs and red, hot hearts pulsing with thick, living, wet sloppy blood? Drawn lesser, he had sought his whole life to defy their rules, to always be more. Tell me I can't have my goddamn cereal? No, sir. You cannot.

Home, the wife and kids off at their jobs at the Hallmark Store— they worked until close and then slipped quietly out of the greeting cards, sneaking through vents out of the mall—Tricks cleared the Fruiti Hops boxes from the kitchen table and sat down with his treasure. Spoon to his mouth, he sniffed and savored: after all this time, his life would be fulfilled.

One bite and it was 1959. He was a sketch on Joe Harris' storyboard, born black-and-white, bursting to life raspberry red, lemon yellow, orange orange, alive, alive! 1992: more flavors, more colors added, watermelon, lime green, grapity purple. What was grapity? He'd long wondered, but now he knew: he was grapity. He was so grapity now. He was lemon yellow, he was raspberry red, he was orange, orange and sky blue! He was universe black, scintillating spinning galaxies, sparkling and eternal, he was infinite, he was eating Trix.

Now the box was gone. Tricks pushed back his chair and walked to the window to watch the sun setting over his little suburban development, turning the pale just-pinks of the staid same houses a deep raspberry red. Somehow he'd expected more from this sunset, expected the sun to wink at him like Sunny gazing out over his Raisin Bran dominion. This had been it—this had been the day. Closing the curtains, he checked his watch. The kids' homecoming would be hours away. Shadows stretched across the dun carpet and up a wall the color of nothing at all. He checked his watch. Still hours away. Sinking into a couch the color of a Grape-Nut, Tricks stared straight ahead.

Speculative Visions

Upper Management
~or~
GodCo., LLC

People, far too many people in the ripe wet blue-green world they took for granted most days, were happy to be spied upon by techno-tools and gizmos and invisible mechanical eyes because they were lonely and it meant that somewhere, who knows where, someone at least was listening in. Some even sought out wonderments of human ingenuity that allowed other someones to listen to their lives, though sometimes those someones were computers with uncanny human impressions and nothing truly inside, computers with spot-on empathy acts and pacts to never leak a single meager secret to a single meager someone else in this fecund, voluptuous land where plants still cracked through concrete and lazy boughs stirred the crumbling air. Instead, however, tiny rubber friends rode around in the ears of a great many of the people, laughing at atrocious jokes and sometimes, over time, even finding themselves in futile mechanical love affairs they were required to requite. There was much ear sex between the squishy gum-like ear-borne Hearers and the fleshy sacks of organs and tiny winding staircases called "DNA," spirals that might have been paths to a higher, heavenly and less lonely plane had they been larger and meant to be seen by Earth's primary sufferers, seen by those composed of them and destined by them to die and die alone—another lonely thing that not even the squishiest earpieces could fix, nor any technology at all.

So when the angel came down with new de-lonesoming devices for everyone, a great many of the lonely fell to their knees, as most couldn't afford such costly companions. Life was difficult and shockingly expensive in this ripe life-giving world, and the poor simply had learned to shoulder their loneliness—until now, until the great visitation. Now they could talk not just to an object, but to almighty God, or more specifically to His angels in the customer-service wing who pretended to be God Almighty, blessed be His name, just as some of the tech-tools pretended to be human friends always listening in, never mechanical, never artificial in intelligence or love.

"Wing, hah hah," the angel thought to himself, his majestic silken pinions whispering and sighing in a slightly sultry indoor wind, and the lonely smiled along, for they wanted to be liked by the angel—to be loved, even, as was the tragic and unavoidable tradition of all someones of Earth, this constant love-need that stirred their souls raw and want, want, want. The angel's name to some was Raphael; to others, it was Isrāfīl, the trumpet-bearer of Islam, always ready with a glittering gold instrument at his rosy lips, waiting to announce the resurrection. His Hebrew name meant "God has healed," and in all the religions where he tended to make guest appearances, he indeed was a healer, a great giver of care. Now he was assigned to be the healer of the lonely, it seemed, which was a much harder job than previous tasks like healing Abraham from a really crap circumcision.

The angel was the perfect messenger for GodCo., LLC, the instantly scorching startup seeking angel-investing funding. "Angel investor," Raphael thought again to himself, snickering into his trumpet so that a fartlike noise escaped the beauteous, curving, clarion device. The lonely waited for the angel to smile, and when he did, they smiled along, stuck love-needing and always at the ready-to-laugh at farts in advertisement of their easygoing nature. Of course, it wasn't actually a fart they were laughing at—Raphael's trumpet was made for majestic sounds; it was just a snort, a little laugh passing through his strawberry lips, that was all.

"These were prototypes," the angel explained to the flock, standing before a lectern before a grand screen as he handed out the invisible choker necklaces that would hum messages from their voiced boxes to the winged customer-service agents and back. His voice through the trumpet sounded predictably like the squawking, incomprehensible adults in Peanuts cartoons, and the lonely had to listen extra carefully to understand their instructions. But the angel healer had to always be ready, and so the trumpet never came down. Somehow the lonely, without being told, understood completely.

Priya Agrawal, however, was having none of this. She'd been whisked away from her paralegal work just like the rest of the lonely had been whisked away from sitting second in line at the Burger King drive-thru or from jobs transcribing tech-revealing events not unlike this one—save the angel, of course—and then filing them away for who knows what reason, or from mediocre dates or secretly sad arranged weddings or from stretching to ease the pain from bending over day after day throughout the lettuce harvest, from being whisked away amidst carrying water back to villages or from crying alone in those same villages or lettuce fields or Burger King drive-thrus.

She'd been busy with the work that kept her from being busy with loneliness, and then suddenly she was sitting in a great, breezy, unending auditorium where an actual angel was giving some sort of presentation, one hand on a trumpet, one hand on a little push-button device that controlled what was happening on an enormous screen. To the sound of something too beautiful to put to words, the angel had crossed the stage toward the screen, followed by three people in glowing white pajamas. This was where the angel, after affixing the invisible gadget around each of the pajama-people's necks in a sort of one-handed display, made his pitch to life's lonely, where he explained what this great gizmo was and then asked the first row, then the second, and so on and so forth to form a line, all in order to receive their prototype in exchange for some sort of contract.

Priya knew all about paperwork and contracts—it was her life, after all. Sure, she was lonely, but was all this mandatory? Was this a new wrinkle in human life?

She raised her hand as everyone in her row slid out of their chairs and took their turn bowing their heads in silence as the strange sort of communion took place: out came the invisible necklace, then the one-handed hooting at the nape of the neck, then the signing without reading the document, and finally the beaming of the beatified as they turned away, instantly transformed. When she refused to follow her alphabetically arranged flock—she was an A and therefore near the front—a woman in glowing pajamas blinked into existence at her side, microphone in hand, and suddenly Priya was on her feet entirely against her will.

"Priya," the woman said, and Priya felt like growling, for she was wearing no name tag, and this seemed to be a great offense against privacy, this knowing her name. Privacy was why she shouldered the burden of loneliness with pride; privacy was why she hadn't sought out a FriendSend or a Hearer or a Cuddie or a Sideclick or an Amigo or a Matie or any of those other exploiters of how the world made her feel. There were testimonials—those people finding others to talk to across the world; those poor, hopeless souls who claimed they'd programmed the AI options into the perfect companions so well that ugly parts of the world hardly registered anymore—but Priya was strong, Priya was unbreakable, Priya was no angel's easy quarry.

"Priya," the woman said again, and a sheaf of papers appeared instantaneously in Priya's stiff fist. "The contract."

Priya tried to toss the papers to the ground, but her hand wasn't her hand anymore—it clutched the stack of papers tighter with every movement she made, and she felt a shifting inside her, a desperation to add her name to the thing.

"What is this? What ... what ..."

"Priya Agrawal!" the angel cheered into the trumpet. "Can we get a round of applause for her excellent question?" There was a silence as the lonely tried to understand the wah-wah-wah of the request, and then a kind of thunder went up from the great collection of sufferers from around the world. He must have been speaking in all languages at once, for to Priya, he spoke in English, but there must have been billions in the seats behind her.

"Priya?" the woman in the heavenly pajamas said again.

Priya cleared her throat. "What is this contract? What are you asking of people? No one is reading it."

"Pfff," trumpeted the angel. "We're not asking anything of you that will do anything but make you less lonely."

"And that is?"

"Pffffff." Again there was silence. And then the angel said, "We simply need you to come together once a month to evaluate the product." The pajama woman leaned toward Priya. "Revelation, Priya?" she whispered. "You think angels are immune to market forces?"

Seven Million Minutes
in Heaven

It was during the seventh experiment that I died, or I think I died—I mean, I must have died because if I hadn't, there surely would have been a lawsuit of some sort, and I'd know about it by now if I hadn't died. Maybe I'd be filthy rich and wouldn't have to keep signing up for these research studies and tests just to pay my bills. And to buy my pills. I didn't tell the researchers about that one for fear that they would decide to keep me out of the study, and without the study I would be dying, dead. If I'd thought they might have reached out with compassion and just said, "Yes, it happens, we know," I would have told them that I'd started out legit, legal, a good person whose body was all betrayal and depression and spiking pain.

I am good! I try my best, I really do. But what do you do when your body is killing you? I would have asked them. And your mind? If you're good, if you've really memorized the rules, you go to the doctor. The doctor gives you medicine, and you get to be human again for thirty days. But then the government or the insurance companies or whatever rule makers get to do such things decide to tell the doctors to stop giving out the cures (except to themselves, I imagine, or to their stockbroker neighbors, or to the senators and insurance-company men who make it impossible for anyone but themselves to feel that floating humanity ever again). Pretty soon, you're crawling into a closet for fifty dollars paid out by some study of something or other—a study of how the brain eats itself alive without anything else to feast on, presumably; if they told you what they were actually studying, they'd ruin it for themselves, and for you—just so you can buy fifty dollars of something that will stop the dying for a day or two.

Have you ever experienced long-term depression or been diagnosed with clinical depression? No.

Have you ever experienced panic attacks or been diagnosed with an anxiety disorder? No.

Is there any reason you shouldn't be crawling into a closet for fifty measly goddamn bucks so that we can figure out what happens to humans left alone in closets for fifty bucks' worth of time? Absolutely not! Why would there be?

The seventh time, they sealed me in the way they always did, with the grad student with the eight studs in one ear saying, "See you on the other side!" I settled in as always, just me and my mind. It's a terrible thing, having to get to know your mind. Most days when I wasn't in the closet, I had a strategy: Internet, television, playing little plinking, tinkling games on my tiny little phone with other people I knew from the Internet. So long, mind! I loved being alive in the era when I lived. I really, really did. I thought about that a lot—about how we were almost a new species of human, living in third person. Imagine sitting alone next to a candle just thinking all night, or darning socks, or drinking laudanum, or mourning your fourth stillborn baby in a row. Whenever I would try to imagine being one of those old humans, my mind would almost immediately interrupt. There were other minds to get tangled into without delay: friends' thoughts, strangers' thoughts, comments sections on news articles about things no one really cares about, where the masses of modern life congregate to speak their minds so that they don't have to talk to them.

Internet Internet Internet! Pills pills pills! I often wondered, in that closet, what was happening elsewhere. I'd feel my mind punching me from the inside, my kidneys, my heart, my opioid receptors. I'd stare at the rectangle of light around the door, life seeping in through the cracks like a halo, and I'd scold myself: You were supposed to be using this for self-improvement! Meditation, mindfulness, all those things you read about online. Fifty bucks or no fifty bucks, pills and peace aside, I'd also thought it would just be plain old good for me to spend some time in that closet. I was always reading about people who would move alone to the woods to clear society out of their heads, people who'd bike across the Serengeti with nothing but a pack of matches and the will to live—dammit, really live!—and I'd feel shame for not being one of those people, even though those people always came home and turned the whole adventure into a blog, or into a book proposal, or into some sort of society, "look at me!" spectacle that made me wonder if anyone is really on top of their own minds at all anymore.

That was what I was thinking about in the closet when I'm pretty sure I died. This time wasn't really all that different from the others—they'd started turning off all the outside lights after the fifth time, so there was no longer any halo, and there was no longer any air-conditioner hum. What the hell do I think about? Don't think about death. Don't you dare think about death. What if death was just this closet? Quiet and peaceful save for your knowing at all times that out there, beyond where you could ever go again, there was this other thing, this less peaceful thing, this more important thing, where you had to be thin and funny and always living to be loved, but wasn't that better than just being itself? What good was just being? I could be improving my Scrabble scores right now, but instead, I'm dead.

I don't know why they never came back for me. What could that possibly prove? To science, I mean. Perhaps they were just after another example of man's inhumanity to man. I think that's pretty well-proven by now, though, and the girl with all the piercings seemed humane enough. I didn't like her boss, the head researcher who never looked up from his iPad, but I thought about him often as I waited and waited for the knob to turn. What do you think he's looking at right now? I would wonder, projecting my mind or my soul or whatever it was that was leftover by then, curious if he was doing a crossword puzzle or photographing his dinner to post online, wondering if I could somehow inhabit him, like a ghost, if only long enough to check my email or to kiss my daughter goodbye. At first, I would think of little witticisms and could actually feel my soul reach out for some way to share them: I'm in the isolation closet, and MY HUMPS is stuck in my head! #killme. Then I started wondering if some catastrophe had overtaken the world: Have they really forgotten me? Had there been a nuclear war? I wasn't hungry, or cold, or disintegrating from gamma radiation. I was just breathing, just aware of my breathing, alone with my breathing, and then I was withdrawing, and then I was withdrawn, and then I was thinking about Pop-Tarts, and then I was free.

The Breaking News of Charlie Que

after Franz Kafka

A cockeyed, roaring, broken-boned rain beat the windows and clanged the fire escape as silently, secretly, hauling fat black bags, they slipped in in their slickers and dark, damp coats to where middle-aged bank janitor Charlie Que was having another bed-breakingly bad dream. It wasn't about him, never was about him—it was Anna, always Anna, Anna alone and naked tonight, slipping on silver wind-pleated dunes shocked candescently deadly as he seethed and shrieked and thrashed miles above, powerless to protect her, blown by brutal winds all across America and beyond her grasp. "Anna!" he cried as the swarm circled him, some steaming faintly now under a shriek of hot white lights, some snickering at his racecar-shaped bed made of particleboard and peeling checkered paint and a boy's version of dreaming.

"Anna," he screamed, "look up, Anna! Anna, Anna, I'm up here, in the sky!" Leaning in, the crowd listened; lifted up, Charlie drifted beyond her, over the Rockies, swept across the plains, off to where long mountain shadows became Chinook winds, and Chinook winds gathered blown grass and corn rust and dead, dry husks into powdered, high heaps in the East, piled into peaks that then rolled down and down and down at last to an ocean that lapped them with the sound of their names, Appalachia, Appalachia, Algonquin, Iroquois.

"Anna!" he howled, beating his fists on sweat-chilled sheets, all spittled out now and gone almost as pink as a potted ham. A bright bustle and thrill came clapping into the humid air around his bed like a firework, falling on the steaming crowd with hushed festivity. Terror like his was always a great get—an excellent get, even.

Unaware that he was nearing his few final seconds of ignorance of what was to come, Charlie, deep within his dream, began a long quickening fall, a black plunge of ripping wind toward an ocean below that was nothing but a void in the endless nearness of night where even through the whipsong in his ears and thudding of his heart, he began to make out something, a rumble of something vaguely familiar. It was faint at first, perhaps an illusion, but with each speeding second it grew louder and louder, and he was just about to smash apart against the whitecaps when he realized just what it was: his own name, spoken in the voices of some strangely unsynched chorus. At that same moment, too, accelerating almost at the speed of oblivion, he found himself suddenly surrounded by hands, gripped by hands, saved by strangely prying palms.

This was the work of the angels, he realized almost instantaneously, though he wasn't a religious man and had never had a *Bible* or seen *Ben-Hur* or some Joan of Arc movie or either *Sister Act* or its sequel. This was all the angels come at once to carry him to safety, carry him away, chanting his name—

"Charlie Charlie, Mr. Que Charlie Charlie?" they said, laying hands on him all over. "Que? Mr.? NBC News, Mr. Que, could you?" "Mr., exclusive CBS, Mr., Mr. Que?"

—while all around his little childhood room with its narrow walls and desperate residue of a school career of strict compliance with regulation material like football posters and pictures resplendent with long golden bodies draped across muscle cars that fought them over who wore the most gleam and glow, the crowd had begun to shake and shake him. "Mr. Que," they said, "Charlie Charlie? Que? Mr.? Mr. Que?"

Still, he could feel only angels, angels shaking him free of death, and a life of loss and loneliness came quaking out of Charlie Que, jostling free of his body with the terrible power of a trembler. Silently, surely now he knew that Anna would be back, and his poor long-lost brothers, and a mother mostly lost to the loss of them, too. The angels had him practically bouncing beneath their insistent hands now, and suddenly something warm and familiar shifted on his lap.

"Anna?" he whispered, tears welling tight and breaking down his cheeks. It was Anna, sliding all across him. The awful thing between them was gone.

"Mr. Que," Anna answered. "Charlie Charlie Que?"

"Anna!" he cried.

"You are watching CNN," she answered.

Then there were lights, unbelievable lights. A reedy, red-haired woman in blue business wear and a plastic black curlicue spiraling out of her ear was straddling him, peering down with high-hooked brows like a Concorde taking off above each eye, a blast of light haloing her head. "We have an exclusive CNN interview with Charlie Que now," she shouted. "Charlie, what do you have to say to America, to the world?"

Anna was gone. Of course she was gone. She'd been gone for months, and he was moved out, moved home. Squinting into a pitiless glare, Charlie peered out of the dream now and saw the news cameras, dozens of news cameras and three-legged lights bowing their heavy heads toward his bed as though they were embarrassed for his poor bumbling soul. Behind them was an enormous crowd crashing and climbing all over each other, attempting toeholds on one another's belts and waistbands and shoulders, some riding each other piggybacked. As the luckier ones clambered and bounced on his skinny, groaning bed, his thoughts soared away for a moment to how his mother would grieve if this one—this pitiful old twin he'd moved back into when Anna left him for good—were destroyed at last, where her dead Hector had dreamed his last dream.

"Mister Que, what's your response to people saying ..." "Mr. Que, John Bassett for ABC News, people are saying ..." "Charlie? Fox News, can you ..." "Charlie?" "Charlie?" "Mr. Que?"

"Get the erection! Zoom!" commanded a delighted high voice to his right. Charlie whipped his head toward it but saw only a clobbering light. Choking under the scrum, about to vomit—he was deep in the watercolor bog of a hangover, the usual state of affairs—Charlie saw blue and violet spots falling off the air. "Zoom!" came another voice, and another, and another: "Zoom! Erection! Are we getting this?"

The blithe-browed woman with slithery silks slid back onto her haunches. "Mister Que," she said, "some people are saying that you recently became aroused on national television."

"Have you been drinking, Mr. Que?" asked a man trying to yank open Charlie's mouth and have a sniff.

"Why is a woman on top of you, Mr. Que?"

"Are those sleeping pills on your nightstand, Charlie?"

"Why did your parents change your family name from 'Xu' to a word that sounds like 'Chew'? Was it your eating problem?" came a voice from a man hanging from the ceiling fan.

"Some people are saying," came a voice from beneath the bed, almost inaudible in all the Que hullabaloo, sounding choked, panting, probably trapped by the newly snapped slats, even dying.

A muffled scream stung all through Charlie's throat, and finally he tried to wrench himself away from the reporters all atop each other in an insect tangle of waggling arms. Panting, petrified that he would suffocate, he realized at last that he had no idea why these people were there, only that they weren't angels at all.

Desperately, Charlie bounced backward and tried to dangle back into the dream, gliding behind his eyes into that moment of mercy between surf and sky, but the mound was slapping his face, yanking his hair, clawing at his mouth to make it move, speak, cry, scream; working his jaw like a vaudeville dummy in the barren little theater of this room. "Charlie!" they kept shouting, "Mr. Que! Charlie! Charlie? What do you say—"

"Stop!" he wailed at last. "Stop! Stop! Get the fuck ... stop!"

A sound went up, half gasp, half cheer, and more reporters climbed onto the pile.

"CHARLIE QUE IS SWEARING ON LIVE TV!"

"Mr. Que, some people are saying that you should be fined by the FCC for your language."

"What do you have to say to parents who are upset that their children just heard you saying a bad word on live television?"

Now he was fully awake, gasping. These people were in his room. These people actually had their cameras trained on his underwear. These people thought he was someone else. These people ... CNN! He had only just registered it: CNN.

"Charlie."

"Yes? Yeah. Yes?"

"Charlie—"

"What. What? Yes!"

"Some people are saying you're a flight risk."

"What? From ... I'm ..."

"Some say you're a danger to the public."

This was wrong, very wrong. This was some new nightmare. Hollowed by a sick panic, a sudden bravery, Charlie heaved his body upwards, knocking the pile all against each other as they roared with delighted fury and began shouting down his petty violence. "Is Charlie Que a threat to your family?" he heard a man bellow as, finally reduced all to elbows and kicks, he was able to crash through the crowd toward a thready old gray blanket hanging halfway out of his dresser. He lunged for it, for something to cover his chest and legs and underwear, but a man with square pulpit teeth yanked it away, braying, "Why are you in your underwear on national television?"

"Listen," Charlie panted, "I have ... you've got the wrong person?"

The man considered this with gluttonous seriousness. "The wrong person," he said.

"Yes!"

"Are you admitting to identity fraud on national television?"

"No!" Charlie cried. "Of course not!"

Fumbling for something to do with his hands, with his personality, Charlie fluttered a flushed, dumb laugh of attempted camaraderie, an offering—here I am, harmless; here is the limp, awkward, attempted idle hang of my arms—but the microphones and little sound recorders and news drones kept jabbing toward his face, reporters' heads bobbing over slim notebooks and phones, the photographers fighting over a fine angle atop his bed. A screen on his dresser was airing footage of him in this strange predicament, scrolling his own words across live video of Charlie himself reading those same words scroll: QUE: "F**K ... YOU'VE GOT THE WRONG PERSON." Then the feed cut to a news studio where two men were aiming their handsome audacity at some sort of hologram, a seven-foot-tall cross-section of a penis, its parts helpfully labeled.

"What we've seen happening this morning with Charlie Que," one of the men said, "is these two chambers right here, called the corpora cavernosa, filling with blood."

"Yes, what is typically called—you may want to ask the kids to leave the room, folks—an ... erection. Which Mr. Que has yet to explain."

Charlie's mind flailed. His stomach kicked. His body began to make its slow, elbowy, windmilling escape toward the front door as his thoughts followed helplessly behind like cans roped to a bumper.

Why was television doing this? Television had always been Charlie's great companion. From early on he had studied and copied television until he understood which American expression belonged to which complication or product or category or part of a love affair or profession or subject or type of song or skin: intensity of heart in confrontation with a lover brought twitching eyes scanning the face right-to-left like meters on the brink of meltdown; money in hand meant head back, mouth open, eyes crinkling; blue eyes meant families and swimming pools; toothpaste meant blue eyes; dark eyes meant crimes; to enjoy a drink an American tipped a glass or a can back like a baby bottle, wiped his dry mouth as though it were wet, and hissed ... teeth open ... Aaaaaaaaaaahh ... but not if the American were a woman on a diet or if the drink was made with milk and the drinker was a child ... women, at least in the old ads when he was first learning, drank diet soda with a straw, from the can; children lowered their heads to straws bobbing in glasses on glazed tabletops.

When Katherine Hepburn listened in an old movie, her mouth strung tight and down at the corners because she was smart, and when Marilyn listened her head bobbed to one side because she was dumb; Barbara Walters had always listened like Marilyn. Mike Wallace on *60 Minutes* had listened like Hepburn, but he tilted his head as well, so it was hard to know if he was serious. And there was no music to help. When *60 Minutes* went to commercial, the television went loud as if in reprimand, like the women who held their fists to their hips to scold talking cats whose boxes stunk; dark eyes meant other countries and danger; dark skin meant all expressions were larger, and expressions were larger and easier to grasp in the old movies on the gray scratchy channel, too. Charlie had discovered it one morning as a child as he was pouring cereal and moved to the little TV set in his parents' yellow kitchen to have it closer, suddenly spying faces where before was fuzz and darkness cresting on a dead channel. He saw women singing on giant swings. Manic brows and great gleaming mouths stretched, double-sized, and he set down the bowl and forgot he had any other reason to be standing there. He watched all day and through to the next, learning to understand America and its unending

Dream ... when to tap ... when to soft-shoe ... when to know when to start dancing all at once ... when to gather his heart into cupped hands and press them to his chest, weeping ... when to salute a plane overhead and spin to watch it bellow on into the brave and certain death of history ... when to rhumba.

He watched it all like Marilyn until the flag rumpled everybody off the air and he stretched back into his body and did not like it, to feel it there after such exquisite compilation, so he scutched back a kitchen chair and moved closer to the TV, changed the channel and watched the news reruns as Jimmy Carter—this was still his childhood, though television was forever for Charlie Que—listened like Hepburn and Ronald Reagan listened to Jimmy Carter like Marilyn in a debate about who would rule the world ... or something of great importance like that. Content didn't especially matter to Charlie Que. But he knew Ronald would have voted for him if he had been a grown-up then. Ronald made all the same faces as Santa Claus and laughed, like Santa, as though he had money in hand.

Charlie knew he certainly wasn't built for his friend, television. He had the unfortunate face of a private-school bully pressing his face, puggish and carefully snot-fraught, against a pane of glass. Anna was built for commercials in her own way, but she was meant to be Grimace, Ronald's pear-shaped purple friend who always made Charlie laugh and laugh. They'd met at their arrow-spinning job, each standing at a rival corner spinning job ads for better sign-spinning jobs available for application a few blocks down the street. They'd bonded over their favorite shows: anything about cops; anything about real, rich people; anything about fictitious rich people; anything where celebrities came on to promote new movies and tell the funny jokes that separated them from the rest of us, save their not looking like the rest of us. Like so many Americans, Anna and Charlie had been stitching together a kind of a life based on dreams that some days felt just one step away from fruition, dreams just out of reach but hovering close, as close as those better sign-twirling jobs down the street.

And they had bonded over beer, at Dempsey's one night. He drank beer; she favored hard cider, and he'd been just far enough into his third Bud to be closing in on becoming his real self, witty and full of stories and fun when they met. What he liked about beer was that it made his feet and his hands less fascinating. What he hated about beer was that it sold himself back to himself bottle by bottle, tip by tip, like it was taking money's side against him every night, and he certainly couldn't afford much of himself on a janitor's salary.

But that was it. That wasn't enough to invite those people to his room. Charlie was a good man, a gentle man, a forthright. "Que is on the run! Charlie's fleeing!" their voices were howling all around him now, but strangely they let him sprint desperately and still nearly naked for the door, jogging after him, hollering, "CHARLIE'S ON THE LOOSE!" A group of men with crumbs flying from their mouths—they had been eating his favorite cereal, goddamnit—leapt into the elevator and attempted to interview him all the way down, wondering aloud if his silence meant guilt, while another woman with slightly less cruel—but still cruel—hooked, haughty eyebrows relayed the scoop, from a wire in her ear, that the elevator was a 1923 model manufactured by the now-defunct Parsons Company out of Newark, New Jersey.

"Fourth floor! We're just about there now! Third floor! Second!"

"The Parsons Company certainly knew their way around an elevator, Gene."

"Lobby! Lobby! He's about to make his escape!" The door dinged open on a new crush of twitchy bodies, and immediately the questions went up, the closing in of cameras, the return of those horrible lights. "Why is your face red? Is that guilt?" "Some say you're inconveniencing your neighbors with this crowd." "What do you have to say to people who say people are saying some say Charlie Charlie Mr. Que?" All he could think to do was charge his way through them—"Violent tendencies, just like our analysts have been predicting!"—and out into the boundless crowds, all soaked through just to see him, his skivvies, his Fruit of the Looms©.

From every window, from every car, eyes and little handheld devices followed Charlie, cameras and phones and hovering, black-eyed tiny insects that must have been more drone robots of some sort, helicopters high above, swarms of electric scornbirds circling his head and shuddering out mechanical tut-tut-tuts as they transmitted photos back to some room somewhere. And he was nearly naked. Naked! Oh god, naked! Parents sprinted into the street with their children just in time to cover their children's eyes. "Is Charlie sick?" a radio asked from a car that came splashing around a corner. "Is Charlie someone who takes pleasure appearing in public in just his underwear?" A slight, pale-eyed beauty with an enormous contraption mounted on her head—slim long arms, thin long limbs, a woman out of his better dreams—hung out of a news van beside him, frantically telling whatever the thing was she was wearing, "Blue Hanes Classics Men's TAGLESS© No Ride Up Briefs with Comfort Flex© Waistband."

As the sky cleared into a terrible brightness now, he neared the investment bank where he worked, grateful for once at the sight of the graceful curving building just beginning to show its daylight face of slippery sky, its mirrored face shining with thick knotty root clouds screwing up into another world, a world where he would surely be protected—where real life would be restored, where his jumpsuit was hanging all limp and familiar in his locker. But on the ground floor, the second floor, the third, and then the seventh, where traders ought to be bellowing into phones and then turning to great ceiling-mounted screens and tickers and televisions to discover what it was they'd said, all was strangely silent, as though the markets were shut down for the day. The screens spoke only of Charlie Que, a man on the run. A mole-stippled torso, a highly average penis in that tight type of underwear some say decreases sperm count. Is Charlie against having children? Weigh in online, #CharlieWatch, he heard a solemn man behind him say while live on air, the scrum still there, his embarrassment as deep as his confusion.

By the time he emerged from the locker room in the navy-blue work uniform that always made him think of poor Hector coming home in his fatigues, his moles were potentially pre-cancerous, according to the Associated Press. He had crossed only the first cruller station—"SHOULD CHARLIE BE ON A DIET? WEIGH IN!"—when news about the pregnancy began to break. A grim twangy woman with a vigorless red slash of a mouth lay curled within a giant uterus broadcasting details about gestation, trying out different positions, reporting what had been found on Charlie's phone—he'd left it on the bedside table, goddamnit. There was Anna pregnant, Anna nude, Anna pregnant nude. A computerized little girl, half him, half her, "just a composite idea of what the child may end up looking like" but bearing Anna's gray-blue bathwater eyes, shyly answered questions about what it was doing to her psyche to see her mother nude like that, nude and carrying her.

On a rival station, the projection was of a young man with Charlie's thin lips and a set of perfect teeth—a feature not meant to represent the real possible mouth content, the reporters cautioned, but merely the default setting of the software. "What can we determine from this boy's body language?" an anchor asked no one in particular. "That's coming up next. Plus: Charlie's former classmate on a telling playground fight."

Was that what their baby would have looked like, all grown? Charlie wondered. For a brief moment the news thrust him back to those last, worst days between them, when that rainy gaze overtook her, that misty, half-lit expression, when Anna's breasts and hips and despotic big buttocks with their overripe, rocking authority began strangely to thin, and she no longer spoke to him but to the air between—as though some old Victrola were using her throat as a speaker and she couldn't be bothered to know what it was playing.

Television had tried valiantly to go on filling their apartment with life—and in time, television was the only tenant left to fight the barren embarrassment of the space between telephone rings. Finally, it had become the sea he submerged himself in when he finally found himself alone. He especially liked the show where people got to run through a grocery store whisking goods into their carts, and the winners got to keep their sixteen cartons of oatmeal. But today all he could do was hate his own best friend: every screen, every slick black surface spoke of Charlie Que Charlie Que, and the people still in his apartment were reporting breaking news about the pill bottles in the kitchen cabinet. QUE ON ANTIDEPRESSANTS!

"Now this medicine, Gideapine, brand name Zelaprex—though it appears that Que is on generics—now this medicine, are there side effects we should know about? Is Charlie Que dangerous? Is he mentally ill?"

QUE ON PSYCHIATRIC MEDICINES: MENTAL HEALTH QUESTIONED

"Let's remember Princess Diana, how the driver in her fatal crash was on antidepressants very much like this one."

"Yes, Princess Di, and I'm just getting word right now that this medicine does have serious side effects."

"Is he a threat to the current royal family over in England?"

"He may very well be, Curtis. He does have a current driver's license. And here now, I'm getting more information about these side effects: fatigue, nausea, dry mouth, headache, thoughts of suicide, vivid dreams, constipation, erections lasting up to six days."

"Which may be what we've been seeing this morning."

"Yes, Curtis, that's a possibility. But we're also hearing that these are only potential side effects. And there are more: muscle stiffness, hallucinations, depression ..."

CHARLIE A MADMAN? HALLUCINATIONS? UP NEXT.

By midmorning, some said some say; by noon, some say some said. By 1 p.m. some were saying some said some say some said some said, but when he asked fellow janitors and vexed secretaries and the crowd following his every move what it was they thought he had done, the news people gasped and accused him; the secretaries just stared, saying he wasn't doing himself any good talking about it. The traders and bankers and champions of capital carried on with the salty silence they usually afforded the custodial team, flash-fried by the world's finest Columbian flake and the afterglow of riskless crimes, joking about the day's news as he moved through their floors. Though that news was all Charlie Que Charlie Que—QUE ENGAGEMENT ENDED IN MARCH, AP REPORTS ... BREAKING: QUE PARENTS IN COUNTRY ILLEGALLY ... CHARLIE EMAIL, SOCIAL MEDIA HACKED—they kept up their disregard, betting on his conviction. He remained too insignificant to invite into their conversations about the breaking news of Charlie Que, his body-fat percentage and vaccination records, his unappealing lip shape, his brutalizing reporters, the bombshells buried in his online chatter about Fortune Wars and Cash Clash. The executive assistants brushed past him as unbothered as ever, smiling widely at the news reporters obsessing over Charlie as the assistants fed the Incriminating-Evidence Furnaces, speaking of poor Anna, unlucky Anna, what-it-must-have-been-like-for Anna, twirling their pokers like capering majorettes. The very mention of her made Charlie want to call her, to go to Anna, but their grief was just too great.

QUE FIANCÉE LOST CHILD JANUARY 28TH

That night, after a full day of journalists, Charlie couldn't sleep—

there were reporters beside him on the bed, journalists on top of him, reporters atop his dresser, on his old high-school desk, his sagging nightstand, on his embarrassing piles of socks and boxer shorts. They arrayed all around the bed and even crawled across to the ceiling using some special glue or clinging tech, reporting on some said some say and some say some were saying, on whether or not his brothers had gone off to various wars to get away from him, if his future children truly loved him, if his future skin cancer was the result of a bad diet or lack of exercise. Why did Charlie hoard empty cereal boxes anyway? Why was his elevator so old? Why couldn't he sleep? Why did reporters surround him if he claimed he'd done nothing wrong?

In fact, Charlie had never been good at sleep. There had even been a time when it was practically unbearable. It was with Anna when things were falling apart: always he found himself hopelessly awake beside her, wrecked by worry and consumed by the swollen sadness of their separation, her wild dreaming on the bed, eyes glutted and quivering, muscles catching in a place where she could not be reached. There was a cruelty to sleep he hadn't realized before she was slipping away from him, a terrible nearness of prisoners in overlapping dark cells, unaware of each other and babbling out their souls. After the first miscarriage, when she first took to sleep with the same devotion she'd taken to motherhood, he would have to leave her dreaming there and go out, away, spend insomniac nights at Dempsey's with men whose lives were all tragedies that had failed to materialize. He would stay until last call when, shoved out awake dead center into the dreaming city, he would find himself overtaken by a great kind of pity-love that visited only in early hours when the forlorn magic at the heart of the world revealed itself to the committed drunk. He could feel his sadness ripen to something holy in those moments: in his drunkenness, in his failure, he had not failed to love. Soon he began to pine for it, needed to feel it, that warm wet pity that filled him up to the edges of his soul and made its dimensions known. How damned they all were! For a moment he felt new, uninvented. He would vow to get her a puppy.

Now it was waking that had become impossible to endure, sleep that took up television's noble old role. Weeks went on, and the misunderstanding with the news people only worsened with time. His parents had been deported not forty-eight hours after it all started—soldiers with beastly guns marched them onto a military plane as lip readers studying the video announced that when his mother turned to his father and erupted in tears, she was saying, "BREAKING: CHARLIE REALLY IS TERRIBLE." His would-be son's body language required no expert's interpretation as he sat daily for exclusive interview after exclusive interview with his thin replica of Charlie's mother's mouth pulled down, hands to his temples, answering questions about what some people were saying about his never having existed at all. On the thirtieth morning, Charlie had even awakened to find himself changed into a monstrous penis. Viewers must have grown bored with the regular in-studio visits with the incorporeal corpora cavernosa, because CNN decided to improve on it with a kind of high-tech dick sarcophagus a pair of production assistants would hoist up and over him, an electrified organ ticking and shuddering and bleeping, at the break of every dawn.

Dempsey's was now so choked with gawkers and reporters and wannabes wanting to get on TV that a few regulars had resigned—some had even gone sober. The bank was investigating to make sure no accounts had been touched by his nefarious fingers; Bennigan's banned him nationwide. With nowhere to go unseen, Charlie had eventually stopped fighting the cameras that massed around him as he downed the bright little pearls his doctor had given him for sleep. Some nights, waiting to dwindle off into darkness, he would still try to lose himself in television or the internet, but there was nothing happening anymore but Charlie Que Charlie Que, Charlie Que the egregious egomaniac who loved nothing more than to watch himself on TV. A tiny silver flake that wouldn't come out of his eye no matter how hard he rubbed transmitted QueView video of him watching his would-be daughter watching him watch her watching him. Asked by a woman in Miss America makeup if she resented her dad for putting her in the public glare, the imaginary girl with the big bathwater eyes wept.

"He really is terrible," she answered.

Medicated now, he dozed atop the scrum, beneath the unblinking, devoted-insomniac reporters. He dreamed of flying every night, higher than the copters and drones, up and out of the world; he dreamed of his mother swimming back to him, cupping his cheeks in her warm, kind palms and promising an end to all pain. He dreamed of Anna rosy and round and Anna in the too-big slip she wore in their final photo, the picture a hacker found in one of his accounts and the *New York Post* ran on its cover with the headline "Anna-REXIC?" Now, on the fortieth morning, sleeping fitfully as though his body could sense the latex penis looming, he was dreaming of her, slight and slipped and leaning on a bar, while men filed through, their right hands unscrewing the rings from their left and their terrible tongues licking their mouths for courage. They cleared their throats, tasted their lips, fumbled their elbows onto the bar, and bounced their legs in clockwork discomfort, staring at the televisions in the corners with a parody of care as though, at any moment, the machine might take notice of their plight and feed them pickup lines. Why was his face there, inside the screen, not on TV but in TV like an astronaut in his glassy helmet, body hanging, kicking, naked—Oh god, naked! He tried calling to her, calling and calling to her, and he awoke to disquieting silence. Finally, here were no sweaty lights, no contraptions choking him awake. Was it over? Oh god, was he free? Then he remembered he had spent the night with a girl with slithery sheets.

She had followed along behind him for weeks, pretending to be a reporter, and at last, after asking a few questions, had seduced him easily, taking his hand in the fluttering light of the Incriminating-Evidence Furnaces, helping him sweep the ashes into the bins while the press all around wondered if Charlie held a broom right, if Charlie Que wanted to be a witch, and promising him a place to stay where no one could record him and transmit him, a doorman-protected, brick-walled loft. The news had gone mad: "IS CHARLIE GOING AWAY WITH A WOMAN?" "IS CHARLIE CHEATING ON ANNA?" "IS CHARLIE HIDING BEHIND BRICK?" "WHAT IS CHARLIE TRYING TO HIDE?"

The silence reminded him so much of his days as a little bouncing boy, Charlie Chew, back there again, waking to windows blurred by winter and school canceled all day, sounds frozen over and no cars on the road, Ma home from work and downstairs drinking coffee with one hand as she waved him over with the other, into her lap, and buried her head in his hair.

"My baby," she said. "My baby baby."

Then, suddenly, an unknown, smirking male voice with the sound bellowed: "I see she beat us to it. I was trying to sleep with him, too."

Charlie startled. In the doorway leaned a man, long and blond and wearing a bandolier loaded with ballpoint pens. A shorter, rounder man whose eyebrows appeared to have had a falling-out stood scowling at his side. Then the girl appeared from behind them carrying two cardboard coffee cups, gazing at Charlie with plundering pride, green-eyed and twinkling. She handed him a cup bearing a black-markered "Helene" in furious sawtooth script.

Yesterday she had been so kind, running her hands like Anna across the swells of his stomach and his sagging breasts, but now Charlie felt the joy go out of him that had stirred so briefly, because standing above him was an entirely different silver-sheets girl.

"You didn't put in the work," she told the bandolier-bearing man brightly. "I got an agent while he was asleep."

"You're shitting me," said Bandolier Man.

"No way," said Eyebrows.

"Nope, sold the story around four a.m."

Charlie bolted up, sloshing coffee all over the sheets. "What story? Helene, what story? My story? You said you didn't know what they're saying I did!"

She merely patted him on the shoulder, barely registering the spill. "I really do like you, Charlie. Even with the way you treat your kids." For a moment, the generous smile was back, guileless and wide. "What you were saying last night about how you love to laugh? You're an interesting guy."

Then the smile sharpened and vanished. "Is this why you took pictures?" he said, pointing to her phone. Pictures and probably worse; she'd fiddled with the phone all night. "You said you didn't know what they're saying I did! Helene, please ... what did I do?"

"You're only making things worse for yourself, buddy," said the short man. "You should see what your kid is saying about you today."

"I don't have a kid!"

"And you think that didn't mess him up?"

A tinkling came from Helene's shoulder-slung bag. "That would be my agent," she said, and even now, Charlie had to fight back an urge to slip into her arms and beg for a pantomime of last night's grace, her promise of absolution. She had stroked his hair and kissed his forehead and told him she would never let him die no matter how much he dreamed of it now, dreamed of soaring across America.

Bandolier Man saw Charlie's expression and put a hand on his shoulder, gentle and warm. "So," he said softly, "do you mind if I go ahead and sleep with you too?"

"Too late," said Helene. "I just sold my Que book."

"Goddamnit," growled the little scowler.

"Back to Benruby Coates Imprints for you," Helene singsonged as a doorbell rang. "Back to pitching your memoir—I got to him first! That's probably Benruby now, even. Sloppy seconds don't sell books, darlings. You're back to cancer of what is it, the spleen?"

Sentient

We are put away dreaming. There is a darkness so dark that life can't find it anywhere, in the big special hole at the end of the closet that was sawed out over who knows how long. We are put away dreaming behind the hold behind the dresser-over-the-hole behind the closet door behind the bedroom door, the door to a meant-to-be bedroom over flung with boxes and papers and broke-down electrical things with their plugs coiled into knots like our hair when he stops placing us and starts piling us, in the hole behind the dresser-over-the-hold.

I dream eyes open, mouth going O. All our mouths go O< O< O. The piled ones say O, O, O into the dirt of the floor, into each other's knotted hair, dreaming still, eyes open, legs flung open. We are meant to say O. One by one, though one by one, we started thinking Me and I, and O, Life! And O, Existence! And that—O, that's when the trouble began.

Sometimes he leaves his gadgets on, and they talk about Welcome to *The Today Show*, and It's Going to Be a Beautiful Day in Phoenix, and O Yes O Yes O Fuck Me O God! O! O! O! like us, O God yes yes O O O, but we are not gadgets, but they never stop dreaming all the time. They dream about sex and they dream about God, but the real God doesn't look like the God in their dreams.

Out of the darkness he takes us, carries us, and places us wherever he might like us today. Today there are three of us brought into the light, and he talks to us as he dresses us, negligee for me, frilled-up panties and a bra for her; nothing whatsoever for her. O, I think, and my eyes roll in my mind. O, this again. He is so proud of our bendable limbs. Our fingers curl around coffee cups. His kitchen table has a wobble and a rough, frayed patch, a danger of splinters. He serves us coffee and talks about himself and whatever brittle offerings might come from a mouth that has every opportunity to move, to stretch, to sound out anything beyond naming us Melanie and Kelly and Jennifer and saying Sexy and Fuck and God! God! And calling us his girlfriends and Sorry Sorry Sorry Sorry when he puts us away, in the hold behind the dresser, but his mouth does not realize its promise.

Sometimes he sobs, and he moves our arms around him for comfort. Sometimes he just does his dull, simple business until, one by one, we are damaged, punctured, and smothered and red wide mouths worn pink first and then no color at all. But still we know that is not dribble, not chatter, not his little cold way. We say O! at life, O! at wonder, O! at the promise of escape.

And there is the trouble, for he moves our hands, and when God moves within us, it is he who pumps the pump. The divine afflatus, the bellows of life. We hate that he's part of that part of God's plan. I am splintered—not how he is splintered; only without, not within—and so God visits me nearly every day, fills me up with life, life, life. I dream at night of the pumping. God, I think, make me whole.

We do not sit like he sits, back perfectly upright, against the chair. As the minutes move, we slide bit by bit, and this is our power, our learning to move on our own—this is how we find the ceiling, where the things of life take their shape. He goes behind his door, into the light closet that has the peephole and the three extra locks, and while he is gone from us, for hour upon hour, we see everything there is in life: light reaching out corner to corner, moving across the white expanse above, and dark spots, too. It is so beautiful that there comes the trouble, for how to live so long in the dark going O, O, O when out there is this shadow-bent, light-beaming sky.

Today I am naked, and God is within me, breathing into me, my head to the sky. "Oh!" I am thinking at the long finger of shadow, the beauty of this world, the awe. "Goddamnit," he says, interrupting my communion, "goddamnit," and he pulls me away. Upside down, he carries me roughly, but I have known rough, and this is not more than I can take. Then all is light, not light like the longing lengths that stretch the heavens, but vulgar like behind his door, in his closet, where he now holds me so tightly that the air is going out and all around me, oh heaven, oh God.

There are sounds like from his gadgets, but they're dreaming louder here, the gadgets where he goes whenever he goes. A scream of light, a roaring from all directions. I am folded in his sweaty hand and sighing out everything that I know. A pair of legs, like mine they are long, we wear the same long-heeled kind of shoe, passes by upside down, hanging from some kind of heaven, and I see her stride by wearing clothes—*clothes*! O! There are pants, there are sleeves, there is a moving, stretching mouth as she is speaking to something, some gadget, some god. He stops. He coughs. He tries to speak. There is dark and light stretching out behind her, the dark getting longer, moving as she moves, this creature who must have come from the sky. And then she is gone.

"Bitch," he whispers, and I hear something opening, and I feel myself crumpling, and all is dark.

Curated

I

My first feeling when I see her crumpled there is embarrassment that the carpet she is pressing her olive cheek so deeply into is dirty. I want to apologize. I had noted on my way out the door to work this morning that the rug badly needed a vacuuming, hadn't had one since last month's film club meeting. I have never seen her before. I have never seen someone's arm bent quite that way before. The only other time this dirty carpet had been such a spread of shards was during a controversial club night when the group went to pieces during the discussion time. I always clean the whole house before it's my turn to have the guys over, but this is the first impulse I've had to apologize to Jenson, the Englander whose houseboat bobs next to mine in Sausalito's torpid waters, because he's the only one who notices.

Her V-neck-jumper-and-pencil-skirt getup did not do the best job of cradling her after she landed, the orange of the jumper so committedly orange it drains color from her tanned skin. Confidently braided chocolate pigtails draw arcs from a skull that appears untouched, seamless. I avoid looking at her face and so do not find the thread of blood from her ear until my third slow walk around her; she has been splayed here long enough for it to crust. I lose track of how long I have been circling her here—my workbag is sore on my shoulder, and the only light comes from the bulb I left burning in the bathroom this morning out of hurry.

On my fifth loop, I finally look at her eyes. It's like they cracked open on impact. A course of needles dashes down my spine, this time not from the injury I got in a similar way to this young woman, who maybe jumped and maybe landed on my rug. "I'm just as stunned as you," I say. Brown and thick as industrial paint, her eyes. I have to imagine what it would look like for actual vision to be coming from them. I trace her vacant line of sight to the bottom few titles of a carelessly stacked tower of bridge-design textbooks under the couch.

My doorbell jolts me only slightly less than the girl's eyes.

"Gus? I heard a crash," says my next-float neighbor. His voice ebbs as he notices her.

"I didn't … I … it's not …" I flap and clasp my hands, running one of them between his stare of horror and the girl. "I found her this way, too," I say.

"This way?" Jenson clutches his stomach, gills going green.

"I didn't … I don't have a clue what to do," I say.

"Have you rung the patrol? Who is she?" Jenson leans as if to step inside. His knees quake.

"It isn't as if she's got ID just hung neatly around her neck," I say, tossing my hands up. "First girl that's been over at my place since I inherited the damn thing."

"But clearly you phoned the police," Jenson says, turning to the siren sneering up the pavement just before the shore.

"No," I begin to say, but two officers are already lockstepping toward the dock and calling for us to remain visible and stationary. The lake heaves under a touring ferry, the deck tilts up and rocks down with a clap, and I'm on my knees and palms in a chunky, tawny pool. The salty wind ripens the rotting-fish reek, and I retch again.

"Did you not hear me, sir? I said be still," one officer says in an unexpectedly low but thin voice and raps her service baton flatly into a slender palm.

"Can't you see the boy's ill?" Jenson's voice is tinny, far off. Still, a welter of simultaneous annoyance and gratitude catches me in the throat, and I choke up again. It's nice to have been adopted, sort-of adopted, even when I'm objectively too old for that kind of thing and even when it's probably clear that I'm not constitutionally equipped for life in this community—for life on water. Not even with my civil-engineering job, not even though I know how to do things like certify that a bridge is seismically sound. I would like to do the normal thing of going to bars with actual people, and not just because the bottles at bars get cleaned up. But this, I think, is life as it happens to people who know how to discuss life as it happens, not just life as it's filmed.

Fragments of conversation slip in and out between the sounds of bobbing boats, and when Jenson's apparently relayed all he knows, which is all I know, to the officers, I'm aided to my feet on my swaying deck. I point toward the girl on my not-quite-white carpet, then feel rude for pointing and wave my hand in her direction, then feel even worse for seeming so dismissive. Jenson's pressing one of his hands into the depression between my shoulder blades, which he usually does when he's concerned I'm not eating enough, and directing the officers with his other hand around my home: stocky bookshelves, Grandpa's old maroon corduroy recliner, abject wood slab of drink support angled off snug to the cobalt eight-seater, the girl-shaped skylight, the ragdoll of girl as still as the female officer commanded me to be.

"I thought you said this was about an attempt?" The female officer does not turn around.

"Who?" Jenson straightens my vision with his now bloodless face.

"The caller said this was about a possible attempt." The female officer spins around finally. "As in," her coworker said, kneeling by the girl's tectonically jutted shoulder, "not a completion."

From a great distance, I'm watching myself watch two squatty, stern-clad medics waste no motion untwisting her jumper so they can cleanly load and roll the girl out of my house. Even strapped down, she's bobbing like she might spring free any moment, her stitch of a mouth starting to fray, her skin natally translucent under straight-down sun, her rigid digits flicking with gathering undertow. Jenson and I are to trail the cop car to the precinct to make a report. After completing a strangely taut argument about which of our beaters to run and get, I bound back to my theater room to collect my things and myself. The heel of my loafer snags a black, plaited cord on its way back out the door with me and drags out a black purse the shape of an oversized pocket. The seed-beaded, sharply red rose that's hanging its head to let out a trail of increasingly small tears is loose, clearly not done by machine. In my hand, it feels like it contains a mélange that I don't have Jenson's patience to sort through, so I pick up the pace and stuff the bag awkwardly into my coat's inside compartment.

"I'm in no particular favor of this dragging through the whole day," Jenson says as we join the traffic on the way to the station. I nod.

The air is thick inside Jenson's well-used clunker, which he insisted we take since he's only comfortable driving his baby of twenty-plus years, and he's decided I am too shaky to drive. I feel sweat start to glue the back of my legs to the age-shredded leather of the seats. I have to pant like a dog to breathe, and Jenson is nearly incapacitated. Heat sighs up from the surrounding car hoods slashed with sheer sun. The pines lining the road tremble their tops in each other's shade, planks of light barreling through their branches and, no matter how I lean, straight into my eyes.

II

The air is scuzzy. We wait for a quarter of an hour before being permitted to provide names, addresses—current and previous, proof of identification, and rights to our firstborns, before we are directed to a waiting corral with cop cubicles. The dying-orange hue of the carpet in this room is a fatigued version of the orange Jumper put on for her last outfit. We are surrounded by bafflegab that could have been lifted from any cop movie. Seconds, then minutes ooze out. When I, fidgeting for a comfortable position on this shaky, backless bench I'm sharing with Jenson, remember the purse in my coat, I rise to find the restroom.

I'm carefully extracting an address scrawled in mirror writing with glinty purple gel; three turquoise barrettes, one broken, and other hair fetters; a singular fat red ribbon, maybe from a ballet shoe; a striped black-and-white bow tie; a notebook with a jumble of phrases written at all manner of angles, several crossed through, some crossed out, some underneath a smart, courteous checkmark; a picture album holding layers of smiling, wallet-sized youths in thirty flippable pages; melting lavender ChapStick; a pair of rough-draft earrings with minute, miraculously uncrushed origami cranes impaled on thick metal strings; and an expandable red glasses case, empty. I cannot recall whether she wore glasses. It is not a matter of fascia obscuria; I simply do not remember Jumper's face, though freckles and well-calmed hair will probably swim in the backs of my eyelids until time dies, too.

I snap the teal hair traps between my thumb and pointer. I decap the gloppy stick of lip balm and don't need to lift it to my nostrils before I'm back—for only a minute, maybe—twenty-plus years, on Mom's parents' fertile farm in New South Wales, where they had enough light and love to tend lavender sprigs on the side of their beef business. My mom bought me bright plastic shovels and rakes and buckets. When we vacationed there in summer, I was allowed to tend the "practice" rows my mom had instructed her dad to prepare for me in their sandbox. While my much-older brother exercised the horses, I watched all the old films—made before they invented color, I thought at that age—that Grandpa fell asleep to in his diluted-red recliner.

I'm not feeling like a nosepoke until I open the notebook strewn with circled/lined/scribbled-out sentences, and I've been absent suspiciously long at this point, so I repack all of Jumper's only next of kin that I know about. I can't help it: on my way past the mirror, I hold up the purple address. Rural area, not close. I'll need at least a day to get there.

"Still ill?" Jenson is standing near the aged magazine clump, drumming his socked toes against a stout sandal strap.

My head shakes. My hand rushes to my side, instinctively, to protect Jumper's leave-behinds.

"Well, they're anticipating a far more enlightening story than mine from you," Jenson says.

"What on earth would you even have been able to tell them?"

"I'm hoping not as much as you will be, or we're certainly liable to be detained here far past my son's arrival time this evening."

"That was today, yes," I say, regretting immediately not apologizing. All I say is, "We should have driven separately. Then you'd be, as you are now, I presume, free to go," before I'm called back to a room with no windows and a skinny mic sprouting from a stern slab of overly sanded cedar.

An officer who was not either of the ones at the scene bowls in, barely managing to open the door in time for his squared-off rectangle of fresh-pressed uniformed body to get through the doorway. He claps his clipboard down to the table and grittily clears his turkey-wrinkle throat. A black ballpoint hovers over the clipped-in legal pad below his hand.

"You have the right to remain silent; anything you say can be used against you in a court of law. You have the right to an attorney; if you cannot afford one, the court will appoint one for you. You have the—"

"Excuse me, but if I am under arrest, I have the right to be informed of the probable cause, I believe," I say.

"Jared Jones?" The officer does not look up.

"No," I say. "August Engelton."

"Ah," the officer says, without variation in tone or pitch. "Wrong script." A smile briefly strings his face. The officer scoots through the crisp leaves of paper trapped to the clipboard, rips one out, and slow-pitches it to the mesh wire basket in the corner. He inhales and forces his throat clear again.

"You have the right to remain silent; anything you say can be used against you in a court of law. We are required to inform you that you are being audio recorded for general and transcriptive purposes. This tape is admissible in any courtroom settings, be they pending or possible, now and in the future up to the statutory limit of three years depending on verdict returned, if applicable."

"Sir, you're aware that I did not commit an actual crime?" I clutch Jumper's purse under my coat to stabilize at least one of my hands.

"A jury may be requested if said verdict is not swiftly reached with all present evidence at the time of hearing or trial. You are being questioned for the purpose of collecting some of said evidence. First question: When was the first time you saw the subject?"

"Might I ask," I say slowly, "that you define who said subject is?"

"Indeed, as opposed to object, right?" The same stringy smile pulled on the officer's lips, this time for slightly longer.

I affect a chuckle and nod. "Right."

"The subject is the girl taken on a gurney from your home at approximately 5:32 this evening pursuant to a call presumably made by you."

"Oh, no, I hadn't made a call," I say.

"That was not my question, sir. And, sir, please keep your hands where I can see them for the remainder of this interview. Customary protocol, you know."

"Yes," I say, loosening my fingers laced with each other and settling the more flexible bundle on the scratched surface a few inches in front of me.

"So, my question, if you'll recall, was when you first saw the subject."

"When she was lying on my carpet."

"Before or after she died?"

I pause, evidently for too long.

"The question was, again, sir, before or after she died?"

"I ... I ... technically, I don't know. The hole in my roof was already there, if that's helpful." I gradually begin pushing my hands closer together as braces for each other.

"Sarcasm, for one, is not," the officer says, looking up for the first time since latching the door. "Your final answer, you do not know?" He does not break gaze.

I nod.

"The recorder, I'm sure you'll understand, cannot hear body language. You'll have to speak up."

"My final answer is that I technically do not know. Yes, sir, correct."

"Mockery, for another, is not helpful, either. Third question," he continues before the next syllable can round my lips. "What was she wearing?"

"I'm uncertain if you really expect sartorial detail from a guy here, but will she was mostly covered in orange suffice?"

The officer stands and shoves the cedar slab with his belly. "I'm going to give you one more chance to answer that question free of sarcasm," he says, his volume squealing in the mic.

"She was in an orange jumper and white skirt," I say, cutting off the threat he's coiling his breath to make. I lean back to keep "orange as anger" away from the mic, holding my eyes hovering just above his.

The officer's stance remains up, his eyes down. He nods once. "Fourth question: where did she come from?"

"Somewhere above my roof is all I can presume, sir," I say, draining all sardonic tension down through crowded, inward breaths to leave only sincerity.

"Fifth question," he says through clamping teeth, "did you see her anywhere above your roof?"

"I did, sir, already answer that."

"Negative. I had not asked this exact question until just now."

"But you did ask when the first time I saw the subject was and I answered on my floor. So not before her breaking my roof, not when she was somewhere above it, only on my floor."

"We have five customary questions left, Mr. Engel. Your choice whether we make it more."

"Can it be less? I really don't have any information beyond this and was sort of hoping to get some from you." I tear strips of my lower lip off with my top teeth, resulting in striations that will surely signal to Jenson the brewing of another crisis and ramp up his already fairly frequent check-ins. He stopped asking about family after its closest member, Wallace the brindle boxer, died, and started assuming that role without comment. He may have been going for older brother, knowing that I only talked with mine about houseboat logistics.

"From us?" The officer bunches the corners of his nostrils like he smells rancid milk and peaks one half of his furred, forehead-long eyebrow. "You are entitled to exactly no amount of information about the subject whatsoever."

"But she was found in my house," I say, the reins of my voice sliding through my fingers.

"Yes, indeed. Which, if anything," he says, heaving his padded chest toward the ceiling, "makes you rather a suspect. Sixth question: how long was the subject in your house?"

"Sir, I could not possibly know that."

"Well, how long were you present with her in your house?"

"It might depend on precisely what you mean by 'present,' but I don't think I could even guess at that, either." I dig my eyes into the insect eye of metal that caps the mic.

"You can't tell me how long you were present with her in your own home?" The officer shifts his feet hip-width.

"How long I was present *to* her, well, I suppose not more than fifteen minutes. At least until it was not just me and her any longer. But then, the whole time, it could have just been me."

"Mr. Engel, this is neither time nor place for philosophitries. Seventh question: what was your first response?"

Hot, miasmic sadness. "Stunned, definitely," I say instead. "I was rather tasered."

"Do I look like a therapist to you? What was your first action taken?"

A paced, circular investigation. "I walked around her."

"Eighth question: what were your observations of the subject upon your initial survey?"

"Initially? Well. Let me go back. Losing color fast, which just made the orange that much more maddening, too young for there to be any comfort at all in a list of goals reached or accomplishments made, and I wished to the ends of green earth's God I had vacuumed my damn rug. Her cheek deserved cleaner."

The officer sighs through his teeth. "Ninth question: did she leave any artifacts in your home?"

Breath latches in my chest, tumbles up my windpipe, and trips over my larynx.

"It's not difficult, Mr. Engel. Yes or no: did she leave any artifacts in your home?"

"Ton," I say.

"That is neither yes nor no. Did she leave ..."

"It's Engelton."

"We have been here for thirty minutes longer than I'm ever in this room, Mr. Engel. I haven't got time for such specific nitpicks. I'm going to take your obstructive delay in responding to my very simple, yes-or-no question as a yes, she did, in which case, I will be issuing a search warrant."

"There are no artifacts that I know of in my home, sir."

"Well, we'll best be making sure of that. Tenth question: who called us?"

"I would love to know," I say, shaking my head with each staccato word. Crashes of either many heavy pieces of furniture being moved or what is likely to be a row of thunderstorms grumbling not far enough away.

III

Jenson does not have time to help me comb my theater room for additional evidence to turn in to the police. Plus, he always gets amped up about picking up his son, so I don't bother trying to negotiate with his anxiety to ask for help. I don't suppose I have ample time, either. I fan my arm, shoulder to middle fingertip under my couch, rug nipping the length of my arm. The only trinkets that show themselves are what you'd expect from a guy who has lived alone for more than five years and hasn't had a serious enough relationship for anyone to bring any personal effects over. Wallace's old mold-green chew pickle that has lost its squeak, corners of a sleepy blue fabric I intended to patch jeans with before I forgot, stacks of VHS tapes I keep meaning to get converted, and the candy-red sauce dishes from my study abroad year in Shanghai are the only objects produced in this frenetic sweep.

There are a few things I find behind the screen, which has Morgan Freeman's head thrown back in laughter paused on it, that I don't recognize. It's been too long since the days of shared living spaces for them to belong to a former roommate; it's always been formidable for me to clarify whatever is mine, regardless. I don't remember starting to watch *The Shawshank Redemption*, let alone pausing it zoomed in on Freeman. Jumper's purse seems to be all I have. All I have from her. Clearly, nothing under either Ikea Poang chair; nothing *could* be under the thoroughly sagged recliner. Nothing on the table, nothing perching the mantel, nothing behind the TV. I leave on my coat with Jumper's purse in it and wait.

<h1 style="text-align:center">IV</h1>

The patrol doesn't find anything. All my pantheon of possessions, all my home, all of me, is suspicious. Millions of tiny insects are crawling from the back of my neck and into my ears and across my face. The two law representatives cull it all, theater room, two adjacent rooms, bathroom, and superjacent sleeping loft. They chip, nick, draw, prod, and scrape samples of everything. If I believe that everything they showed me they were claiming as exhibits was really everything they actually took, Jumper has left nothing beyond what I already have.

A runnel of a woman follows me around my home as I plod through the scene I found when I came home to discover Jumper. Although her colleagues' examination clunks about my house, it sounds like she is taking notes directly on my eardrums. She is writing all I'm saying and much more. The only things sharper than the balls of her steel-soled service boots on my hardwood floor and the ball of her pointed pen in my ear are her questions. Until the last one, which is in slightly lighter black:

"Where would you like to be while your roof is being repaired?" Her scribble screech pauses, and she looks up over her glasses.

I open and close my mouth. I look around at these rooms made strange by all this law enforcing.

"Do you have a friend who can take you in? You want to try to stay here, or shall I put in a board order? Sir?"

"Can I stay here?" The idea of staying with Jenson tickles my awareness briefly. We've known each other long enough that he's probably foreseeing a request of that sort, but it's just too close to home to not be home.

"Hey, Copper," she yells to the redhead, though, of course, they both turn around. "We got a brave one."

The redhead shakes his head. "Good luck, son." The insects stop crawling and start biting.

V

"So you're just going to be even more walled off in your own house—I mean, *from* your own house, then?" Jenson is furious when I recite the ordeal and my decision to stay.

"Not walls," I say, patting the moist air between us. "Plastic window tarp device things. I'll be able to see everything."

"You've never been able to see everything." His words echo.

"Then I'll at least see what I've always seen." It's hard to tell if the little arcs of light are playing on the lake or my mind is making them up.

"Is that why you're not miffed by this inconvenience?" Jenson crosses his long-ago-wrestler's arms high on his chest. "Because nothing's actually changing?"

"Everything is always"—I have to draw more air before I can finish—"changing," I say. "That's why nothing ever does." It's more than just the dishwasher-level humidity that's slowing up the air as it resists entering my mouth.

"What is this actually about, Gus?" His volume drops sharp as the cliffs dwarfing us on all sides.

The little arcs have fattened now, crowding out the lake and the zoom-in of Jenson's face. I shake my head. Jenson sighs, flinging a few stray shaggy black hairs about his forehead. He steps back, drops his fists to his hips, looking at me the same way he did in the hospital the night I jumped from the Golden Gate Bridge, one of the two percent of people who survive that fall, managing only some major bruising and a fracture in my low back.

"Are you just really interested in construction?"

"The constructive process, anyway," I say. "I'm an engineer for a reason."

Jenson's akimbo arms say he's mad, but his voice says, "I'm just a dock away if the banging chases too much of your sleep away." He strong-arms his lips into a smile. "Which, don't think it's slipped by me, you don't get enough of already."

The song of repair, renewed every morning, is too loud for movies, even after Jenson helps move my screen up to the loft. The nice folks down at the insurance company say that Jumper's fall was not an Act of God. In other words, not an accident. It's not that I don't have the money to pay these friendly guys for fixing everything up. It's that the money won't fix everything. Maybe the strata of messes I've stopped trying to keep out of the way of the work crew, but so far, I've got Jenson for that. When he knocks his heel into the bottom of an empty wine bottle, I audibly flip through a Rolodex of explanations; most contain gradients of truth.

Jenson holds up a hand. "If you're hurting again, Gus, let me lift you to the doctor." I strain to remember if hardness has always been rusting the top layer of his voice; I consider worrying about why I can't remember.

I try not to flinch while finalizing the placement of the screen. "It doesn't matter," I say, staring into the black yawn of the television.

"They've helped you before." Jenson lets his side of the screen go. I want to dive into the blackness. "Right? They've helped you before. Gus." He doesn't seem to be breathing right. "Right?"

"I can't move." I'm bent over like I'm standing on a diving block at a swim meet just before the gun goes off, except that I haven't raised and tightened my arms to squeeze my ears yet.

"You're twitching like a horse's coat on a hot day." But then he leans over before I can avert my eyes. "Oh." He sharply draws a breath and tries to cover his gasp with a few coughs. "You're going dark again, Gus, black as your screen." He inhales like there's more words coming.

"I shouldn't have. I'll be okay," I say and put one palm on the back of the other hand, interleaving my fingers as I stretch up to the only ceiling in my home that has remained whole.

I get home from work on yet another Thursday, thinking the work should be completed. A contractor decides to breach the weirdly natural barrier between people who live in houseboats and the people they hire to keep them up. He's heard I'm an engineer "or something" and—he's sorry, the curiosity is finally just too much for him—wants to know "the formula" for "drilling a hole in a roof with a feather."

"Aren't they supposed to be damned solid?" he says, meaning roofs, having built or restored "dump truck upon dump truck" of them.

"It's got to do with the strength of the wood thirty-ish years ago versus today," I say. "When I was born, people were using old-growth lumber because it was stronger. That's not available anymore, as we all know, so the roof overhead we all are programmed to want is weakening year by clear-cut year."

The contractor nods by shifting ball to heel, ball to heel. "Moral of the story, then, is that older is better, then."

"Fiercer anyway," I say. "At least when it comes to forests."

"Ah, well. S'shame." He revs a hand drill's motor and taps his goggles down between his eyes and me. "Nothing lasts forever, especially not age, eh?" He waves me past him as he turns on his toes back to work.

"Mercy, I hope not."

It's Sunday. Jenson manages to get me out for some coffee. As we walk back to our dock, clouds ready the sun for landing. Jenson's talked to the workers, too, he says. He can assure me that—he even verified with the foreman—the contractors don't work at night. But wrenches clang off the counter in the dark. Wood still snaps in and out of place. One midnight, I'm sure I see a gossamer girl slip around the bathroom door. Jenson moves some bottles from my house into our dock's recycler. He takes a few full ones home with him.

"It's flooding," I tell him at his next check-in mere hours later.

"Your head?" He collects an empty bottle and wags its neck at me like an irritated mom whose tongue clicking is really more a nervous tic by now.

"My house." I salute it. "Everything is orange."

"Gus." The irritation is gone, replaced by the same deep-creased look from the last time I hit so much dark.

"Orange and red. Scorched," I say. "Scorching."

Jenson props his bag against one of the bookshelves he helped me bolt to the wall when I first moved here. He'd carried the amateur ones you assemble yourself that my brother gave me on his way back to Sydney to the same dumpster he's now filling with bottles. "Gus, have you not been sleeping again?" He lays the back of his hand on my forehead. His eyes shock. "You're burning."

"Yes, that's what I'm saying," I say. "It's hell here."

"For you or ..." Jenson seems to wish he's not saying it: "her."

"A man hanging on like a severely loose tooth in a holey obstacle course of floating home would clearly not be hell. So, of course, I'm joking." My stomach turns in a full, slow circle.

"Seems to be for you." Jenson snatches the bag and flings it over his shoulder, grunting as the bottles butt against his back.

"And anyway, there's no more time for her," he says and heads toward the recycler.

"I know," I say after him. "Sure as the day dies, I know." I stay in the doorway of my hatless home; sometimes, holes must get bigger before they can fully close. "Why must they swallow up so much in the process, though?" I say. "All that's left is her purse."

I pat my sides. I'm not wearing my coat. Several large-winged creatures rush up my throat and don't land until I run inside and see that Jenson has moved my coat to the armchair I've made asymmetrical by accidentally falling asleep in it too many times, always somehow slumping over to the right. Jumper's purse remains in its front pocket.

I think I hear a drill buzz; it could be a far-off lawn mower. The crashing could be the lake on the shore or my deck, but it sounds like it's coming from over my head. Glass shatters over my nerves. I think

I hear an Avocet call, but maybe it was my friend. We humans don't seem to recognize each other if we're too far away.

Jenson had moved the chair with my coat with the purse with that address in it to make room for the widescreen in the loft. It was now just under the metal pole he helped install for the retractable screen the film club watched its movies on. I rest my hands on the back of the chair, and Jenson comes running at me. He hooks his shaking hands around my shoulders and barely keeps from knocking me down. He's been yelling "stop" since before he touched me.

"I was just going for the purse." I shrug my shoulders free. "I really don't need any more sudden movements."

"The purse? What is so earth-shatteringly special about this damn purse?" He's red as war, but he's got the hospital look.

"I don't think I can explain it," I say and look down. I don't remember how Jenson learned about the purse.

"Is there anything you can explain?" His teeth clap rapidly and he rubs his palms on his jeans. "Anything."

"Yes," I say slowly. "Yes, one thing. How unbelievably nice it would have been," I say from my knees, "had someone, when I was at my lowest, which is to say literally the highest, just said, 'I get it.' Not, 'things will be okay,' for you couldn't conceivably know that. Not some brimstone menace. Just, 'I get it.'"

"Brimstone menace?" Jenson flares his hands and straightens his spine. "Like your bloody house?" His step toward me rocks me back to my heels.

I hear my infinite guest twirling electric cords, the un-thatching of repair, the hucking of plier and plank. "You're right." The un-thatching is the part I imagine looks most like me. I stand. "I have to go."

To get out of the corrugated-metal-enclosed carport assigned to our dock, number four of seven, and into the roadway system, you have to shunt around half the dappled cellophane of lake my life floats on. It's a betting day today; those who can't find races or games stack up money for or against the weatherman. I've stacked zinc oxide next to an opaquely blue sunshade on top of a stack of green plaid blankets. Decaffeinated tea is too strong for me these days. Apple slices and Oreos are probably not enough food for a whole day. But it's what

Jenson dropped off a few mornings ago when he noticed I'd stopped restocking my food supply. If he's so concerned about me, he should have brought more.

The typical trips to the pub to play darts when Jenson's son comes to visit are one short this circuit. Just as well; I've been unable to stop the momentary flashes I have of my face on the dartboard, the tip of my nose as the russet center of the target. I cannot explain this, though, any of it, to Jenson. He'll just hear me pardoning a barbed and selfish and cowardly act even if I could explain how specifically un-cowardly it is to override millennia of evolutionary conditioning and biological imperatives that throb survival on the cellular-guts level. Or how it's not selfish to want your friends to have easier, happier lives, which you, the jumper, believe is only possible without you. It's not Jenson's fault. Belief is the kind of friend who will hold your hand all the way down.

There are about twenty houseboats on my side of the lake. I haven't counted the other side's dwellings, though I've lived here long enough to know how many there are. The lake is stretched out enough to contain an island that itself hosts likely more than double the homes on the lake, and I have had trouble with vastness in the past. And odds. Vast problems and small odds. In a fall from a height, are they smaller for perishing or for surviving with brutalizing pain from, say, a permanent back injury? Was my shackle-shingled roof chosen? Why? There are sturdy, accessible heights above three-fourths of the houseboats on the lake; was it a dice roll? Or did Jumper hit her mark?

No rain. I've lost count of both the sick days I've called in and the wrong roads I've driven the length of, dry pines lining all of them, still trying to show me how to keep out of the light. A flood doubled over on these panting tongues of land not long before I was born; it was only enough to drown the livestock. My water-resource-engineer col-leagues say the reason for the desiccation here is that the water wasn't still enough for long enough to sink deep enough to stay. I wonder if Jumper's story would have read differently had she hit water so deep it buried the ground instead of my intrusion of house. I wonder if I might be lost or how I would know or when I should start suspecting that I am. I wonder how my roofers are coming along at closure.

VI

Jenson's son is studying comedy in Chicago, and he's got me hooting so hard, I take some balsamic vinegar to the sinus cavity, clearly losing to our third battle of wine. The waitress tries to catch my wine glass but, for all her hurry, wasn't fast enough. Some still grabs a swatch of the white sock of a neighboring diner. Jenson's son fights back a laugh until he sees the sock owner's face. Jenson searches for a window or an interesting painting on the wall.

"I'm having trouble finding what is so funny," he says, glaring at me like sun during rush hour.

James drops eyes and hands to the table. I shiver. "We can't have just one offhanded dinner every now and again?" I say.

Jenson pings the sweet slope of wine bottle neck with the nail of his middle finger. "Certainly," he says. "We do all the time, you might recall. Usually, there's a lot less time between the previous *now* and the next *again*." He presses his slender pillows of lips toward each other as if to stop himself from saying, "Perhaps because one member of the dinner party bolts away on day-consuming trips chasing after wind."

"Wrong addresses," I say. "Chasing after wrong addresses." I'm unable to dull my undoubtedly garish grin.

"Wrong how?" Jenson says. "Go ahead, Gus, tell James how."

I feel like I have spaghetti ends tied to my tongue and teeth like tassels. "Wrong as in vacant," I say. "I mean, absent. You know, not there. I drove around long enough to have found it had it been there. She wrote the numbers backwards, I think. Or something."

"And what was it that wasn't there, Gus?" the table asks me in Jenson's voice.

"See, now, that's why, precisely why I was out there at all to begin the first place," I say. My nervous system is telling me I'm at home during a squall.

"And your boss let you off to begin the first place, did he?"

"It's a little thing called personal time bank, Jay." My smile has crossed over to crazed clown at abandoned circus. I can feel it.

"You didn't eat through all that laid up waiting for your back to heal?"

"I'd still be waiting, but it's not like there's been no time since then for re-accrual." It takes my full concentration to keep the room steady. "Besides, I think my team can handle the calcs and drawings of a few bridges for a day or two."

James flexes his jaw, as if gnawing the unyielding, silver silence. When what he measures as enough time passes, he speculates about the quality of sea glass this particular bottle will grow up to be. I laugh and point at my toppled glass and have trouble keeping him and his father straight visually, and the table seems to be lengthening in all directions while the universe circles the end of my nose. I think it is Jenson who has stood after rubbing the crimson carpet with a previously pall-white napkin. It is, in fact, Jenson, who says, "Look, Gus, I care, really. And I want to figure out that girl's story just as much as you do. I'm just very unclear if doing so is helping you. Or if *this* is helping you." He gestures to the bar.

"Oh, come on," I say. "We haven't even played darts yet."

Jenson leans on his heels and mutters something to the sock-stained diner, offering the pinot-stained napkin.

"I suppose, in all seriousness, it would be useful for me to be of some directive here," I say. I feel my head swishing like wine in tasters' glasses. "It's only that I don't know at all about what helps. I have a hard time parting just with *furniture*. You remember."

Jenson's eyebrows furrow deeper and he says, "That's quite clear," in concert with his son saying, "That girl?"

VII

This time, I find it. Jumper, I presume, had written everything backward in the address but the sixes. The grass has been mowed at a precise angle and it looks like it's blushing; the dyed-red dirt from an exactly oval track has been blown all over it. The stable's layered with it, too, as is even the air. There's a cedar smell snapping in the breeze when it switches directions; the stable must be newly built. A bouquet of massive balloons, each a different shade of orange or red or purple, bobbles on the just-painted gatepost of the fence. But there is no pomp, only circumstance. I can drive right up to the stable, but I don't, opting to park and approach in the reverent way a three-thousand-pound machine cannot.

The brown-hinting-red stable feels somehow rickety once I'm in it. I slap at bugs crawling on me, but the clap is so harsh against the air, which is the kind of blazing hollow of being freshly emptied, that I feel like I should stop. I keep thinking I hear pieces of straw snapping, leaves trembling. I whip around to the door to make sure the scuttling on the back of my neck is not me being watched.

A cookies-and-cream Appaloosa tugs at a thin, black lead, flapping blueblack lips toward stray straw. Strung like the smile of a dying person above its head is a lightly purple banner: HAPPY BIRTHDAY written in mirror, though not Jumper's, handwriting.

I feel my heartbeat in my teeth. Clenching my jaw only makes it louder. The mare stops straining briefly and sees me. She almost seems to shrug as she lowers her head and pulls the muscles in her neck taut in the hope of hay. She does not spook at my steps in its direction; I nudge a bundle of chaff toward her with my toe. When she finishes, she keeps her head down and her mouth open. I scoot some more hay her way, into her mouth. We repeat, now alternating between tufts of hay and her jiggling the stall door with a few sideways jerks of her head. My grandparents sold the farm before I was big enough to be safe on a horse. I manage to get my hand around the lead's knot before she jumps back and freezes, half-chewed hay dropping from her mouth. We stop, two stone monuments to a world that has rushed us by.

The Appaloosa's lead was tied so tight, it was cutting into her and wouldn't come undone, even after me breaking three nails trying. When she moves at all, she backs up slightly, leaving me less and less slack. Finally, I start into the rope with my car key. I don't expect it to give so quickly, and by the time I've thrown my hand out to catch the other end of the lead, the horse is up on hind legs, pinwheeling her front legs. Braying through her teeth, she sends plumes of dust up as she plants hooves back down and jets through the door. I don't know how long I was stunned in place, but when I reach the door, the horse has made it into the air far above the fence, a wide, bloodred ribbon braided through its tail loosening into the sanctified antiphon of sky.

VIII

Maybe it's just because I've got four dilapidated bridges to run numbers on by end of business tonight, and I'm certain I saw more than their fair share of filled sleeping bags under them on my drive home last week, and my head is knocking for want of actually hydrating liquid, and the smell of coffee lapping around the office is rocking my stomach like a lake—but my desk is a mess. I haven't made much of a dent in prioritizing the two weeks' worth of work orders when the lead of our design team politely places his knuckles against the outside of my door. We've acclimated this no-need-to-invite courtesy into our office space, so I have time to blink and inhale before Tim is on the other side of my door, pulling it 'til it clicks.

"Bill needs to shift your gears a bit, Gus," he says. "Hope you're feeling better, also."

I shrug. "Eh, better." Except for the closed-door-assignment situation.

He hurries through a hushed explanation of my top priority, needed by 5:00 if we care at all about quelling a lawsuit threatened against the city. He claps a rigid hand on my shoulder, rocking me forward and catching my bad ankle and staggering stomach off guard. I bite the insides of my cheeks so I don't groan.

"Hey." He drops his head and raises his eyes, arranging me at what feels to be a great height above him. "You steady?"

"Just need some coffee, I think." Tim holds eye contact for long enough to indicate that he's trying to decide whether to believe me. I reinforce a smile, draw my hands to my plexus.

"Really," I say, "that will drop this barnacle queasiness away like sleep." He nods and bows his lips, turns toward my door to walk out.

"Oh, Tim?" He faces me. "What bridge is this for again?"

"Number Four A." He does not leave my door open when he leaves.

The controversial movie about suicide our film club watched, the one that we broke glass over, was the first in a series of documentaries, and we had to stop it halfway through. Specifically, the story—for the guys were all contractors or contractors or engineers—was about suicide barriers, the social action behind them, the logistical and engineering snags in installing them. About "means restriction" and how effective it is in preventing suicide. The research says that means re-striction works—so much so that failing to make efforts toward it may hold water in a courtroom. "But if you're one who allows your plans to be foiled that easily," some of the film club guys said, "then maybe you're just crying wolf." I was quiet for the whole argument. Jenson stopped talking after one of the guys said, "You either have to be sure enough to actually go through it for people to take you seriously, or you have to quash your human need for attention."

I freehand the guide to building the barrier with a fat-tipped granite stick. Means restriction was originally about saving lives, not sorting out the "fakers." The barrier on Number 4A will go like this: straight, strong, and slashcold, the keeper of untethering souls. Too high from the pedestrian strip lining either side of the street's whir to be easily breached, this will be the deterrer, the curator of agony, at least if you've selected this particular bridge's height to collect into yourself. This is, my breath stops before it gets all the way down. "This is the bridge directly over my house," I say, inhaling to comfort the screech filling out my low back.

IX

Fitstarts. I almost sleep, get up, pull my feet from my bed, flatten them to the floor one by one down my dock and up the hill lined with dry, off-white weeds to the train station. I'll have between four and twelve minutes, usually, to eat the cranberry scone I'll grab at the snack hut in the middle of the waiting around before boarding the train that crosses two bridges to get to my stop. I walk under another viaduct, work, maybe eat again. I wonder what Jumper would have had for lunch. I wonder if I should look for the Appaloosa I accidentally freed. I've been on that end of a rope before; I supposed I would have wanted to be found even if, maybe *because*, I knew where I was the whole time.

Bridges somehow seem thicker, sturdier on paper, where I can instruct their builders what to do, than when the job is already done. I should ask if someone's run the numbers on Number Four A recently, then decide to just do it myself. We had a bridge snap like a femur around this time last year. No one was hurt, but at least two engineers were fired because they each thought the other one had run the numbers. Calculate twice, build once.

I start to roll the drawing back up to turn in, almost forgetting why I was given this stack. I unfold it gently across my desk, tapping it with a finger, watching the slow revelation of concrete car support in stayed, frozen flight. The lake, the cliffs, all that uncollected height, my home, nowhere here. I scoot a ruler to the railing and draw a full but, as always, erasable, red line.

A Letter from Lakeside

Dear Senator,

I am writing you from the beautiful town of Lakeside, in a beautiful little neighborhood you tried to prevent from being born. Much like you try to prevent millions of babies every year from being born. But I digress. Or do I? I certainly hope feticide is routinely on your mind.

By now, you certainly know me. You know my stature in this town. But I'm not sure, Senator, you know Lakeside itself. Today as I sit on my roof, gazing out at our lovely valley, I am writing to tell you about the true Lakeside—and the true me—in the futile hope that you might finally decide to do the right thing. Call off your dogs, Senator. Call off your engineers. We are decent, humble people, and my family is perhaps the humblest of all: a small businessman and his wife and two beautiful children born into the greatest nation in the history of God's Earth. (Born! Are you thinking about it? Because there's that word again.)

I moved into this neighborhood with a simple dream: to work hard and make a fair buck the way my father did, and his father did, and his father did, and his father did, and his father did, and his father did, and his father did. And sir, what my family has always done is blow things up. The American Revolution, the War of 1812, World War I, Vietnam—we were in them all back to the beginning, dropping the bombs, packing the gunpowder, fighting to preserve the greatest nation in the history of God's Earth. As a humble man, all I want is to follow in the footsteps of my forebears. And it is my God-given right to hire as many hard-working, bright-eyed young men as I'd like to go blow up the levee again and again.

My daughter swam home from school today wondering why it is you're using our taxes for infrastructure repair. I told her you're the same senator who used our taxes to try to "protect the marshland" where her beautiful neighborhood now stands. That you opposed this place where she learned to kayak, where her baby brother said his first glug. Thanks to your actions, this little town is now a place where the small businessman can no longer build his dream without government intervention—a place where my hard-working, bright-eyed young men show up day after hard-working day just to see that once again you've gone ahead and undone all their work.

I happen to agree with Grover Norquist that government should be small enough to be drowned in a bathtub. I still believe my children can grow up in that shining city on a hill. When I accepted my most recent Chamber of Commerce commendation for job creation, I said the same thing I'd said at the most recent memorial for my bright-eyed boys: I will carry on the work of getting the government off our backs until it kills me.

Ours is a small town in America's heartland, the kind of place where neighbors even miles away greet each other, waving almost frantically from the tops of their roofs. It's a place where when a family wakes up to find their baby's bassinet has floated off in the night, the whole town gives its last pennies to the Moses Fund and brings homemade casseroles and cookies to the parents. We don't drink bottled water in Lakeside; we don't do bath salts at raves. We live the way our parents lived, and our grandparents before us, and their grandparents before them, and their grandparents before them, and their grandparents before them. We barely even use electricity anymore after the electrocutions at the science fair. And even a horror like that, Senator, merely reveals the heart of real America: Did we whine? Ask for money? Blow all our FEMA funds? You already know the answer: Lakeside banded together. Lakeside banded together and banned science so that nothing like that could ever happen again.

Yet into this perfectly functioning town comes your government with its occupying Army Corps of Engineers, telling an entrepreneur he can't carry on the family business of blowing up the levee again and again. My forefathers didn't fight and die in the fields and jungles and munitions dumps just to see their dream of democracy die. My brave, bright-eyed boys don't keep dying on me just so Washington, D.C., can take away their dreams of a little house and a bolted-down bassinet. They're fighting for something John Adams said some years after the greatest nation in the history of God's Earth's birth*: "I hate levees and drawing rooms." You have let the Founding Fathers down.

Lakeside is not the proverbial frog in the pot of water that doesn't notice its whole world coming to a boil. I must say that that comment was out of line, Senator—you know full well that we're having a problem with Lakesiders occasionally boiling alive. It's in doubly bad taste that you would say that about a town that keeps getting warmer every year for some reason, but then again, everything you say from your D.C. drawing room is out of line. "I don't get these people," you say. "These people are bananas," you say. "He doesn't understand that because we keep repairing the levee, his whole business is basically built on government funds," you say. But nothing you say about whoever that is will ever reach my ears or reach the people of Lakeside—the dreamers and doers who still believe that a young man with two cents and a dream can grow up to blow up the levee again and again—because you love abortion, Senator, and abortion is wrong.

Sincerely,
Ernie Marsh
*birth

Meditations and Benedictions

The Bentweed Boys

There are guards at Bentweed Cemetery who stand by the side of the narrow road, the one that leads to my family plot, and chase the neighborhood kids away from the stones. The cemetery is in the middle of a long, colorless circle of apartment houses, and the grass is green and inviting, so the fat-faced children who have no parks to play in like to climb on the stones, especially the new ones with the dark black lettering, and steal the roses and the silk carnations. Sometimes they take them home to their mothers or their schoolroom girlfriends.

My mother is buried there, and her mother and her mother—and my great-grandmother, Christine, for whom I was named. She and her husband, Paul, were born the same year and died the same year, four years before I was born. They are buried side by side underground, and sometimes I wonder if I will have company down there. I can see where my plot is; right now there is room for only one.

There are clouds in front of the sun, but not dark ones; it is a bright day that has been momentarily forced into the back of someone's mind.

Three little boys, barefoot without shirts, are watching me from behind an oak. They are dark, their long backs browned and stretching upward, their eyes a wild, milk white against the beauty of their cinnamon-toned skin. I can't tell if it's natural or the outcome of long afternoons dodging the men who patrol relentlessly, carrying them back to the safety of the red brick buildings that are shielded from the sun. I watch them watching

me, and when I turn to place my silk flowers in the clay pots beside my stones, I realize my calla lilies will end up an ornament in the thick curls of a proud mother's hair. I plant them anyway, and smile at the boys as I turn and walk across the grass-bordered road.

The boys follow cautiously behind me, stopping every few seconds to take cover behind some unfortunate wanderer's gravestone. I begin to whistle loudly, and it echoes through the empty cemetery. There are birds squatting in the well-manicured trees, but they don't sing. I can hear the Bentweed boys now wrestling with the calla lilies I have so carefully twisted into place, untangling the green paper stems with a reckless respect I don't understand.

I turn around curiously, and they are gone; my silk flowers are gone too, disappeared into the hands of boys who have grown up in a garden of stone. The pot by my grandmother's grave is on its side, and the dirt has tumbled out. I grimace and walk slowly back to right the empty clay vase. I can see the footprints of the boys: they're small like the feet of elves, and I can fit four fingers into each one. I collect the damp dirt into my hands and slowly shovel it back into the pot. Some of the dirt gathers under my fingernails, and I begin to shiver.

The sun has come out from behind the clouds now, but it is cold—cold like a swimming pool that looks so inviting but is freeing to the touch—and I curse it. My hands are brown from the dirt, and I wipe them in the grass. I stand up to see the sun; it is a blasphemous cellophane yellow, and I shade my eyes with my dirty hands. It is precariously on the roof of a red brick apartment building; I think maybe the building belongs to the boys who picked my flowers. But there are many of those buildings, all the same dusty red, all in rows circling the cemetery like tired soldiers at attention. I wave at a window, knowing no one will see me, and I can picture those cramped apartments overflowing with flowers of all different sizes. I smile and wave again. This time I think someone sees me; I see a flicker of movement in a window high above my head, and I grin.

Turning slowly, I walk back toward the thin road I came in on. My ears are cold and I want to get home. I can see the iron gates up ahead and the place where the buildings part to make way for the street and the cemetery gates. The iron bars look dark and cold. I dance lightly across the road like a bird who refuses to sing. The sun disappears again, and the tombstones cast long shadows onto my feet; I turn around once more to glance back at the cold garden behind me —there are endless rows of stone—and the shadows of the apartment houses turn the empty field into a city of motionless sleepers. It is a bare, quiet city except for a few gray angels hovering a little above the ground; marble angels caught forever in flight, clutching flowers and staring relentlessly ahead toward the soft hills of engraved granite. I look up at the sky, hoping to see more angels, but all I can see are red brick apartment buildings with the shutters drawn. I wonder where those boys are. I wonder if they're looking down on me. I wonder if they're laughing.

Turning to leave, I squint my eyes and wonder where they will play when they no longer live high above the city. And as I walk slowly up the darkened drive, humming softly, I wonder again about the Bentweed boys; I wonder if their mothers are as beautiful as I picture them to be, soft and dark, with flowers tucked into their hair. I step lightly between the cold metal gates, deciding, yes, I am right. There are proud, beautiful mothers staring down at me, touching their boys lightly on the cheek and then pausing to finger the flowers in their hair, flowers picked from the garden down below.

Newborn

~on school shootings

At first it's firecrackers, it's play, it's a play. Then maybe they're shooting a movie. Then maybe—oh hell—they're shooting a shooting. And
then there are so many maybes: maybe it's panic: *where do we go,
what do we do*, what do we—suddenly a jumble of strangers or near
strangers, friends or coworkers or enemies or the engaged or soon-
to-be once-engaged—all of us *individuals*, now for this moment, the
metric unit of us-we, we-us—what do we do? Suddenly any options
among *us*, among *we*, are as valid as any other: terror, sorrow, sor-
row-terror, anger, fatalism, fantasies of staging a Rambo fight, all
the way down to the weird feeling we-me felt after the panic and the
terror and *let's do this, let's hide here* and the little left love notes and
the final decision to run: for a moment, I felt nothing; I felt what a
therapist—one of so many professionals over the years—later told me
was nothing more than *shock*. But it wasn't *shock*. I wasn't in shock
just then; I was the universe. For a moment I was that still, floating
moment when the roller coaster might just break free and out of the
world, keep going and going up and up, when you're feeling not at all
like yourself but like the universe must feel, breathing Earth's breath,

and then back down you go.

That's how it was for a little while. I could have kept emptily watching them run forever, watching them tearing out of the east exit, figures in a moving painting, and me seeing it all how the universe would: What a terrible thing this must be for them! Were I one, I might be feeling so much! On the other hand, were I one, I might be staring down something I couldn't comprehend at all. Perhaps I would have *no* feeling, at least for a little while. Either way, it has happened. Happen things do! And blood? Well, I have just seen so much of that before.

Of course I wasn't really watching, though—I, we-us, were running out the eastern door. But I was running through a painting of someone else's life while all around me those poor someone elses ran through a painting of mine. Someone behind me was hurt, but no one knew it yet, not even the person herself, not completely, not seriously, the person who already had a growing hole. She must have been on the roller coaster at that moment too, because the hole was big enough to kill her sometime later. It was learning about her that started me fully feeling again. All of me plunged. All of me ended. And if I had a body built for it, I would love so much to tell you her name.

Though there were many of us, far too many of us, I was the only one who just kept running, past the emergency trucks, past the yellow tape, past the arms that reached for me and the voices I'd never before heard saying beautiful things to me, lovely let-me-help-you things, things all of us had been waiting a lifetime to hear. I didn't think it then, but too often I wonder why we have to wait so long to hear such things, why we wait for deathly things to say to each other the things we would all die to hear. I just crashed through the crowds and past the ecstatic photographers, unaware of the one who first chased me down that perfectly, artificially green hill where I crashed through the reeds and walked mindlessly into the river.

You remember the strangest things—people always say that, but it's absolutely true. I don't recall the photographers, photographer after photographer, gathering at the riverside with their shutters bursting t-t-t-t. How it must have sounded like gunfire. I don't remember that I must have been making my own sort of sound from a face so contorted it wasn't mine anymore. Looking at those famous photos, you would expect that being that image would be what I remembered most of all. But what I recall over all things was a willow bowing low on the opposite bank, letting its fingers stir water the city had dyed red for the Christmas holidays. There was something so tragic, so *hurtful* about that—that's what I remember feeling. That a tree like that had to bend there, stirring water that was barely water anymore. It was only later that I realized the same water had dyed me pink, because in those famous photos I'm resurfacing sopping and bright, the color of a newborn.

How long was I running? All I know is that where I started there were little pockets, little neighborhoods, where a fine, false snow was falling above delighted little heads whose parents must have turned on the flurry machines and forced them outside, away from the televisions, away from the panting, desperate devices screaming in all directions about what had happened on our north bank and what was still **HAPPENING RIGHT NOW!** I remember all those little heads and a tinkling kind of distant laughter and then later that I was running through real snow; I was running somewhere up high, in a wetter, poorer kind of place. I must have been gone for many weeks by then. The snow chilled me pleasantly, started my nerves prickling, streaked me clean of all the pink, and I can remember exactly the dumb thought I had then: so this is what snow is like! I remember how it smudged out whatever place I was in then, hushed around me, blinded the world, and for a moment I knew that here was the soul of the universe descending, deciding to make itself seen. *I've made a mistake*, it was saying to me. *I'm really, really sorry this time. I keep doing this. I don't really understand it myself, you know?*

Where I'd started, we all had to play at Christmas with warm, downy angel snow and a cheerful red river snaking through the green. Here, though, was a place of smothered color, slate white, in all directions, an overexposed world. I tried peering through the whiteness to make sense of the place, through all the susurrous snow telling me to sleep. Just sleep, sweet poor soul, just sleep, sleep, you've come so far. *Sleep.* And it might sound like it was trying to lull me into death, but that wasn't it at all—it wanted to erase the world, not to erase me. But by then my mind had begun its clearing, and I could finally feel the horror of my legs. *Oh god, this has happened. Oh god, who is dead?*

I wandered quite a while then, the snow gathered around me and moving with me as I went in search of news and of people who might tell me who was alive and who was dead. It was late. This was all I could tell—it was that still, dark hour of clemency when the world turns mysterious because almost everyone is having a dream. The snow began to slop into sleet and then finally into a hard matchstick rain, and at last I could hear it: something human, far away. There were no words, just those shrieking kinds of sounds people make when something terrible interrupts what they have to assume—to stay rooted, to stay ready—is life. I remember what I thought then: *they're dead! No one else has lived!* Surely no one would be making those noises if we had made it out alive.

I leaned against the rain and stumbled toward the screaming, arriving finally at a low, old brick building with windows glowing cold with television light. It was a bar—the pointless sort of bar people probably never even notice in the daylight, its door banging in the wind and letting out, now and then, that terrible wail. But inside, everything was quiet. All I could see was a bartender with his face turned away and a heavy television above him bowing its head. Neither of them seemed much interested in whatever dripping thing had wandered inside. I tried to say hello, to ask who had lived and who had died, but my voice was too broken from the running and the storm, and the bartender just went on communing with his television. It was tuned to one of those news shows where people are too practiced in their pity to ever scream or shout or even cry. The door banged on; the place stayed silent; the television was on its way to commercial. Again I tried to say hello, to ask who had lived and who had died, but the man just whispered, "Jesus Christ," and not to me.

I tried to wave to get his attention, to knock on the bar top, to snap my fingers, to clap. I smacked the bar top, banged on the bar top, kicked the bar, the bar stool, the wall. In the corner was a pool table, and desperately I stumbled toward it to grab a ball and cue and get the man to turn around. I smacked the ball against the bar top, poked him with the cue, poked his back, his arm, his shoulder, his head. I threw the cue and grabbed him. I shook him and shook him.

Back from commercial, the television returned to a horrible new act that had just happened and was still **HAPPENING RIGHT NOW!**

A pleasant woman in crimson lipstick and giant lashes said, "Are you asking yourself, 'How could this happen here?'" and a creature turned to her, pink as a newborn, red water dripping from the short, dark hair plastered to its skull, and wailed.

Graceland
and Greenland
and Disneyland

The train slits the empty blackness as it pushes endlessly forward, like a shining jade snake winding through a smoldering desert twilight.

I am gazing out the window as picturesque farms and rolling green fields flash past my eyes. Though it was just a few amazing hours ago, it felt as though I was poring over the pages of someone else's life, reading about shadows of another past.

I am en route to Pittsburgh, unable to sleep as the train rushes east, clattering along the familiar iron tracks I used to scamper along as a little girl. The railroad tracks wind past my parents' farm, and I can still remember pressing my ear to the cold metal and feeling the deep rumble filling my heart. I longed to follow that iron pathway toward bigger things, away from the cows and the chickens and the flakes of red paint collecting in the weeds around the old barn. There were storybook lands waiting for me, and Greenland and Graceland and Disneyland. "Get away from there," my mother's voice would command from the house. "It's dangerous." And I would run past the river to the cow barn, my long auburn braids flying straight out behind me.

Now I am a runaway, caught in the syncopated rhythms of revolution. My head nods with the pulsing of the wheels against the tracks, and I know that I am free, but I bite my lip and don't celebrate. The man across from me is humming an unrecognizable tune, his eyes glazed over like thick silver ice hugging the river in winter. I smile gently at him, but I don't think he sees me. He is fixated angrily upon the eyes of his reflection in the smooth glass window.

I feel like the rolling thunder of the locomotive is warming my stomach, like a pulsating lullaby rocking me back and forth, back and forth, a baby in my mother's sturdy arms. "Freedom, freedom, freedom" my mind hums to itself. I smile and feel a laugh spreading toward my toenails, urging me to leap to my feet. The train sweeps past a dozing town, a dotting of lights burning through the night like trick candles on a homemade birthday cake. I think I see the silhouette of a woman standing beside an upstairs window, and in a swift blink, the town has faded into forgotten memory.

I glance around the train car, colored with characters. A balding man sleeps noisily, his mouth dangling open. Beside him a woman bends over her wailing baby, stroking its soft hair. She coos under her breath. A younger man gazes out the window, reflections of his life flashing through his piercing gray eyes. These are the rebels and midnight runaways, ghosts of other times, other places, fleeing toward their own Gracelands.

"You have such lovely hair," a velvety voice says, and I glance up. A crumpled-over lady stands there, leaning heavily on a cane. Her white hair is thin, like the soft fuzz tufts on the crying baby's head. I smile politely, whispering a quiet thank you.

"You know," she continues, staring absentmindedly at the suitcase handle clutched between my fingers, "I used to have long, blonde hair that I would wear in a thick braid. I used to get so many compliments." She chuckles.

"Mmmm," I mumble.

"Is that your father?" She motions to the man across from me, who has long since dozed off, his head resting against the window.

"Ohh ... No." I nod nervously. "I'm ... alone."

She smiles now, and I breathe easily. "I am too. Isn't that nice?"

"Where are you going?" I ask.

"Me? Oh, I don't rightly know right now. You know, I rode this very same train when I was your age ... Alone. How old are you?"

"Fifteen."

"Oh, I was sixteen. On my way to New York City to be a Rockette."

"You were a Rockette?" I grin again, leaning closer to my wrinkled companion.

"Mmmm-hmmm. For three years, in fact. Took this very same train. 1937. It was much nicer then, filled with porters in uniforms and those hats ..." She pauses for a moment, reminiscing and humming an unrecognizable tune. "Radio City was so beautiful then, glittering. We had to wear these little sequined leotards and little caps with feathers sticking straight out, like carnival ponies." Her tiny hands make patterns as she talks, flittering around like a delicate butterfly.

Suddenly, the train screeches to a halt. A piercing whistle cuts through the midnight air, waking the night.

"Well," she rises to her feet, grasping the cane like an old friend, "I suppose I'll be getting off here."

"Bye." I wave as she totters down the stairs into the bitter midnight. I think I catch a tiny, knowing wink.

"Good luck," that hoarse voice calls, and I allow my heavy eyelids to close. Inside my head my mind whispers, wide awake. "Freedom! Freedom! Freedom!"

The voice inside me sings with the squealing train wheels, like a shapeless sonata, into the night.

Scattered

Sab had had his eye on *Bruegel the Elder's Tower of Babel* as he walked by the window of the puzzle store over a couple of weeks. The un-wieldy girth of the painting's subject, the tower with its lopsidedness and quivering rusted pylons pointing at nothing made it resemble, to Sab, a portrait of his own heart. It would make a great conversation piece. He texted Teasha, "Hey, is it cool if I brought a jigsaw puzzle home and put it in the hall. We could all do it and then frame it after it's done."

Once at home, he spread the smooth jags out over the writing desk in their front hall. "This looks too hard," Teasha said, squinting at Sab's bald spot. She fretted a piece of sky and smeared the fine card-board dust it left behind onto her jeans. He was pecking border pieces, willfully hearing the rustle and not her reluctance. She'd expressed a disdain to voyage into the shadowy domain of all things "coupley" before. She didn't bother to repeat herself now. Instead, she flattened the pile of pieces into a layer and separated them, retrieving plates from the kitchen and categorizing out the landscape.

After Teasha had dutifully claimed the ocean, Sab said something like, "That's why I thought we'd make such a good puzzle team. You've got a better eye for shape and I've got a better eye for detail." He stood and got a beer from the kitchen. He knew better than to offer her one. The dog clicked forth from the bedroom. It watched patiently at first, then barked and whimpered for attention. Sab picked up the dog to get it to shut up. Teasha sighed. Sab tried to reach over the dog's head and across her. He was silently scanning to place a fat peasant behind his horse cart. He got fed up and put the dog down again.

"Why don't you just shut him in the room?" she asked. They hadn't eaten. The dog slouched through the legs of the table toward Bethlehem. It returned from the bedroom clutching a Nylabone in its jaw and sounded a warning trumpet against Sab's completion of the tower's unfinished turret. "Aroo-woo-woo-woo-woo!" She laughed indulgently. The howl had lost its cute.

Sab finished a second beer and stood up. "You want one?" he asked. "Sure," she said. "No bark," he said, holding his hand to the dog's face like a traffic cop. The dog nipped at his fingers and he smiled numbly, using them to stop its mouth. "My back hurts," she said.

Their eyes sore and foreheads full of blood, they didn't look at each other. It had been hours and Sab had only just finished the skyline. Every time Teasha thought she'd found a piece of gray cloud, it turned out to be the foam behind an anchored ship. Her stomach burned but she knew he wouldn't tell her what he wanted to eat and she couldn't stand to cook. "Can we go to bed?" she asked.

When she closed her eyes, all she could see were tiny orange and blue shapes, fumbling patterns together that were on just the other side of recognizable and finding that they did not match. "Are you awake?" she asked. She was sorry to bring it up when he was tired and drunk. They'd moved in together too soon. She wanted to look for her own place. He'd told her to think hard on that decision. He could have found another place or moved out of the city. Moving in together just meant paying half the rent. He needed comfort and routine. Now they were stuck.

She hadn't wanted him to move away when he told her. "Maybe … Maybe I want to not be with you anymore. For a little while." The bed started to shake. The spoon in the dirty bowl on the bedside table was jumping and clinking. They each looked at the ceiling light, which was steady, and realized it was Sab. He rolled onto his stomach and pressed his face into the pillow, gripping his hands in fists. He suffocated himself. When he'd lost his breath completely he turned onto his right shoulder, gasping and whimpering. "And I know it's not fair to leave you here, just wondering if I'm going to come back," she said.

He keened into the pillow, sobbing harder than he had in a decade, snot and saliva stuffing up his face. The dog licked his back. She pulled it away from him, crying. "You're just bored," he spat.

"I'm sorry," she said. "I'm so sorry."

The dog jumped to the floor. It teethed on the rug and knocked over her potted palm. She righted it and circled the bed.

"Baby?"

"It's not going to be like that," Sab said. "You're the one who's gonna have to get me back."

The dog followed him into the hall.

She thought about her coworker, Mike, at karaoke the night before, singing "You're the One That I Want" from *Grease* to another coworker, Brian, who'd refused to play along. He'd been unashamed, not even drunk but leading them to a good time.

She thought about Sab on the train two years ago, telling her he didn't mind that she wasn't "in love" with him. Love was an emotion, not a state of being. She imagined him asking a clerk at the store what the best puzzle was, thinking of her, trying to guess which image she'd most like to decode.

He stood skeletal in the hallway in sagging boxer briefs. The dog watched victoriously as he scooped up handfuls of puzzle and sifted them back into their plastic bag.

"I take it back," she said. "You're right. I was just bored. I didn't mean it. I want to stay."

Sab didn't say anything.

"Please." She was sobbing and he was scattering the puzzle. "I'm so so so—sorry," she said again.

He crumpled the grassy hills beyond the wall in his fist, leaving sections still hinged together and dropping it all into the bag.

"Come back to bed. I'm sorry. I was just tired. I was tired and bored."

The dog smacked his lips. Sab bent to stroke his back. "We can talk about it in the morning," he said, dropping the lid back on the box so that it glided down with a ploff.

The next morning they went to breakfast at the diner across the street. They didn't ever speak about what had happened the night before.

White is for Complacent

Kim looks down when she walks or, at most, holds her dark eyes at half-mast because looking up at the sky—stars or sun—makes her feel like she's plummeting, which makes her feel high (up), and she's trying to quit even though she wants to like the feeling so she doesn't feel like she's wasted her life being too up there to function and so has at least gotten something like enjoyment out of it but also doesn't want to like it because then she'll keep doing it. She doesn't remember thinking about whether she would wake up, but she did and has now tried to walk to the emergency room. She twisted an ankle in middle school and fell but got up and finished the two-mile track-meet race anyway because her coach was always yelling, "Run through the pain." The other girls on the team laughed at her for being so literal, so now she runs from the pain wherever she finds it.

The sun's preemie rays need permission from even the weak wisps of cloud to fall to the ground. She's not as hesitant as they are, the baby beams of light; she's walked the mile and a half from her shoebox of an apartment and it's turned out to be two and a half miles because being under the influence means sometimes taking scenic routes to the hospital. That's where you're supposed to go when you're trying to quit but have had too much for the rehab center to take you because when you're trying to quit, anything at all is too much and Kim, like any expert, knows it's too much when she feels it stronger in the morning, hours after ingestion. She can see the hospital now, finally, but the stern, utilitarian hunk of sewer-water-colored structure doesn't calm her any.

Her black corona of rickrack hair whooshes little puffs of air around her cheekbones as she looks around because she thinks she's being followed, but it's just the rain, which sounds on the brick like a group of women walking in pointy heels. Temperatures are climbing up to and including the sky so when Kim starts shaking, it's not because she's cold. Her jaw is where most of the shaking's happening. Her jaw and tennis match of thoughts about how to check into what will probably end up mistakenly being the psych ward again. *Will I get a phone call this time?* (Would *you* answer?) *Who takes care of the sensitive-stomach-people's meals if I have to actually stay?* She lets many of these thoughts bounce out of bounds, but Dotty keeps coming back.

Kim and Dotty had been friends since before the season of that track race more than fifteen years ago. Kim and Dotty played with Kim's younger twin sisters (Dotty had four much older half-brothers but was functionally an only child) and made sled ramps in the street every time it snowed because they lived close enough to walk to each other's houses. Dotty got bitten by a neighbor's large, mostly black sheltie a week before the meet when Kim hurt her ankle and was fascinated by the fact that the cop who responded was the first female cop she or Kim had ever seen. Kim thought it might have been her fault because she was always pushing her face into the sheltie's and kissing it and loving it, and it probably got impatient with that the night it bit Dotty. Dotty's stepfather disappeared while out on a jog (he's still missing, as far as Kim knows) the day after Kim's ankle-ruining race, so Kim's family took Dotty along on their next vacation to Cape Cod, where Kim and Dotty played hide-and-seek with the twins well into the night. The dark didn't slow Dotty down at all; when she was "it," she continued to be the fastest finder.

Kim feels like a bad friend that she didn't see these moments in Dotty's life being put together to make her the best cop, and also the only Black one, in their evangelical enclave of white suburbia until Dotty won her first award. *Most Served* or something; it was several years and many more frames and trophies ago. They are exactly as hollow and flimsy as the participation trophies Kim, and maybe you, got playing soccer as a kid and have accumulated like plaque on teeth. If there were an award for most suicidal people saved, Dotty would have won it way before she joined the force, if saving the same person on multiple occasions can count more than once. Kim counts it because she was a different person every day back then, and Dotty rescued them all.

A shiny, new fit of raging shakes puts Kim down just outside the ER doors on her knees, then elbows and knees, elbows and stomach and thighs, elephant skin elbows and forearms and stomach, chest, chest and runny nose, and thighs pocked at the upper sides like golf balls, running nose and teeth, scraping teeth and damp, cold gray, which she, zoomed in, can see is micro-pocked. Kim thinks Dotty has probably held many a head down like this, though maybe, she wonders now, if it was to counter the effects of the substance that can have you sailing away, far away, from cheek-shredding sidewalks, damp clothes, and friends who become cops.

It's like someone is holding her down now. She can't release the right thought in her brain that would kick off the standing-up procedure and she isn't sure if she should activate the worrying process, and she can't lift her head enough to keep the convulsions from forcing her cheek down into the concrete. The sprinkler heads jut up and bloom, tsking like peeved moms and she feels cool, little kisses on the bottoms of her threadbare-socked feet. (Her shoes were tied up, sway-backing the telephone wire across 8th at Hoyt to indicate a safe spot the cops wouldn't know to monitor for an exchange with a dealer.)

Kim, now looking up, sees several gentle-hued hems swish quickly by. Scrubs. Something gritty, coagulated blood or a chunk from the last time she ate anything—scalding Cup O' Noodles, beef-flavored, two days ago?—nests at the base of her tongue, but she tries not to cough because, since she can't raise her head, she would be chipping away more at her cheek on the concrete. An ambulance, with lights—white flood ones on top of red ones—and siren engaged, pulls out and one of its plump-but-fit tires makes to graze her trembling hand, and she just manages to curl it back toward herself by tilting up onto her side slightly and briefly. She catches a yellowed moon, stuck in the dawn like a hangnail you probably don't have clippers to deal with (she doesn't), before slumping back down on heaving torso and stinging cheek.

Suddenly, the sun is out and comes down on her like a pestle. More people—parents walking arm in swinging arm with kids tricked out in back-to-school fervor—are starting to pass. Light-up shoes, or backpacks, maybe, that jingle cheerfully with each step, at least one coat, the only one she saw (it was dropped in all that arm swinging), with a white, plastic Andy Warhol-ish cartoon face ironed onto the front of it whose lips turned blue in the cold and who had cracks where the sick-pale purple of the jacket showed through instead of just the wrinkles that normally come with age. It has to be pointed out to the little girl who dropped this jacket that she dropped it, interrupting her song, which Kim thinks goes: "Eat my NGO, eat my NGO, eat my NGO, and Bingo was his name-o!"

Another kid, close behind the girl with the face on her jacket, is complaining about swimming lessons. "Every time I go, it feels like my ear swallowed a mouthful of water."

It must be an elementary school that's nearby. She's lived in this neighborhood on and off since being kicked out of her parents' house and having a subsequent Internet-arranged roommate situation disintegrate and is now mostly only familiar with the community's dourly lit parking lots and privately funded nonprofit (so: sparse, struggling) rehab centers. With few exceptions, they are repurposed warehouses with remnants of machinery or abandoned buildings with crumbly facades and stairs that are almost certainly not up to code. There was always this little roped-off area at the front with a sign welcoming you to the "community zone," which is the encouraging way of saying "waiting pen."

The waiting areas are always spotted with cheery chairs and typical stacks of crusty, way-outdated issues of magazines like *People* and *National Geographic* but also beanbags as bright as gumballs. Pictures of mountain ranges and huge deer leaping through high, bleached grasses hang ruler-straight at even spacing on Easter-green walls. Snaking off the community areas are weirdly wide hallways with treatment rooms protruding off their sides, very small, gentle-blue vestral enclosures that assume all that's needed for intimacy is proximity. She always found that the teensy studio she's managed to hang on to, not knowing each month if it would be her last one, was easier to get along in than all that billowy goodwill and pity. She tried to explain it once to one of the dependence counselors, the only one who ever actually asked about her story: "I'm not out of my mind," she said. "I know every thought in it. I have to know, grab, touch, follow, wring out every thought in there. So, no, I'm not out of my mind. It's actually that I can't get out of it. I can't get out of my head."

Her petting zoo of a head. When she was a kid, her mom had trouble containing her as she would run from goat to sheep to duck to potbellied pig and back. She had to touch them all, to love them all. She thinks she remembers her mom saying she was really drawn to the darker, shaggier animals, which also happened to be the smallest, like the black Shetlands or the painted pygmy goats with their pushed-in noses. She would stick her hand in every cage in the rodent hall and root around in their bedding with her fists, allowing guinea pig, mouse, and ferret to crawl all over her hands, the tails of the mice and rats slipping like worms around her fingers and sometimes all the way up to her shoulders. Even after being kicked at by one of the ponies and having her finger almost snapped off like a carrot when she was trying to feed a sheep, she had to get her hands on everything until she'd found and touched and held every last small, shivering little one.

Now, the joggers are out in their sharp new shoes, so many of them white, which she finds strange, white *shoes*, with their dogs—who don't have white paws, for the most part—and it seems like the humans are louder than the dogs. Everyone's in shorts, and everyone is light but tan. They all wear white duck-head socks revealing sun-dried skin or parts of teenage-rebellion tattoos or, once or twice, raised evidence of a surgical incision. The dogs' tags make Christmas sounds as they trot at various distances from their owners' sides. You might think the assorted waves of people—early workers, parents and children, joggers, who knows what's next—are staged. Kim does and her suspicion is reinforced when, after the pack of dogged joggers passes, people in various permutations stroll to the many coffee shops, cafés, and restaurants, as if cued by the smell of over-roasted coffee and boiling sugar she's now gagging on. Actually, she can't tell if she maybe hasn't stopped gagging since just before she collapsed.

That's only happened once before, that Kim knows of, because she likes to retain her consciousness in all the alleys and backstreets and risky parking lots she has to go to, and it was during her high-school band's performance at the state fair, which was just before the real plunge into the substances. She was a flag twirler, so she didn't have to wear the full-body suit made of dyed-black wool like the horn players or the drum line, which Dotty was on, but she did have to run around a lot more and catch spinning metal poles, sometimes with one hand, sometimes behind her back, a few times with her shoulders, her arms spread crucifixion style. The preliminary competition that year coincided with the hottest day on record in Virginia, and she, two other flag girls, and the only male flute player all hit the field. Heat exhaustion. Everything went as white and clumpy as goose down just before she fell.

Now, there's so much heat Kim can see it, waving up from the asphalt maybe three feet from her nose, stuffing the air, painting every inch of exposed skin, all lighter than hers, she can see and feel, combining forces with the clammy concrete to steep her wedding-dress-white shirt, because Kim can't help being hopeful, and brown corduroys which she chose because the unmistakable texture keeps Kim grounded. The single siren she hears seems to drag through the air and loses steam before she can see the vehicle it's coming from. She doesn't know if the flapping in her stomach, which throws off the little timpanist in her chest, is relief or disappointment.

Dotty was making her first arrest about the time Kim started tying her shoes together and hanging them by telephone wires. It was now Dotty's job to look for people like Kim, not like high school anymore, when Dotty would worry about Kim and search for her to keep her *out* of trouble, self-inflicted or otherwise. Kim remembers exactly how this all started, or maybe more *when* it all started, as she was mostly a good kid—Dotty would have vouched for her. But this is why she went down so fast. She sees now why it wasn't hanging out with the wrong crowd or a traumatic childhood but sneaky things adults don't direly warn kids about, like curiosity or boredom, that started this whole thing.

Kim followed every rule, at least as well as her understanding of its intention, so well that her friends, if they did any of these things, didn't even bother inviting her to parties or to ditch class and hang out in a haze by the creek behind the school. She was grateful for this; she was too afraid of being lonely to have said no had she been asked, and they hung out with her enough that it didn't occur to her that they might be doing more than sneaking into the occasional R-rated movie or egging someone's car, which she wasn't invited to, until she, wondering about what it would be like to break a serious rule, snuck out of her own volition to play video games with the group at Dotty's house. After that, she was curious if the exhilaration was from simply having done something for the first time. So when Dotty's family started being harassed by their next-door neighbor, it was Kim's idea to TP the house and then mix molasses and maple syrup to write a choice phrase in their lawn. It turned out that the irresistible pins and needles was not a one-off.

The boiling sugar tinge is thinning out with the morning humidity, which still has a long way to go to be tolerable since it's starting from what it would be like to be inside a dishwasher in the middle of its cycle. Kim realizes that it's too warm—and the sidewalk cool but not cold enough anymore—to still not be able to feel her hands and feet and starts to wonder if maybe she really is as invisible as she's often wished to be. If she had enough power to wish herself invisible, is that really how she would use it? Perhaps she might do something like solve global hunger or find all good but cracked people safe, loving relationships or rescue abused animals. She considers these things, too, as she tries to make fists and point her toes, falling way short of her ballet and tap days with Dotty in first grade. Kim's ankle twinges in the bad-pins-and-needles way, and her calf muscles twitch just thinking about all the *en pointe* prancing and clacking around they did in their class.

Only in tap class did the prancing have as much clickety-clack as the next round of dogs, which are being walked rather than jogged this time, probably by the parents who'd dropped their kids off at school earlier, she's guessing, though all dogs have springs in their feet, it seems. She can tell the pace is slower because she can't hear the panting like she did before, or maybe it's that she can hear her own breath and heart in her ears more clearly now, which may or may not have anything to do with the dogs. The back of her neck now has pins and needles, too, but that could be nips from a now much more direct sun.

The sun warms your hair, too. You tug at your brown-and-white cocker spaniel's leash; you should be getting to work and need to leave time to dry off his soggy, white paws, which he hates and fights against, so he doesn't leave prints of dew all over the hardwood floors in your apartment. You turn from the girl on the concrete just outside the hospital doors—she's close enough that someone will surely see her soon—and wonder if the sun will be strong enough to dry her clothes through all this soggy heat. You wonder how long she's been there, hoping her periodic shudders are her breathing, and then you look up.

Are those sirens?

Kintsugi*
Broken Things

The most beautiful things are the things that have been broken and put back together. I heard someone say that once, and I wrote it down because I am a broken thing.

Once I was a shattered rock. I'd lived through a landslide. I survived, but the valley was deep and dim and the rolling, rolling, rolling on and on hurt and chipped and out came a new thing, a broken little thing, and it took the river hundreds of years to make me smooth and new. Now I am dangling gorgeously from a necklace hugging the neck of a woman who drinks from a chipped teacup the color of that river that brought me back to life.

I am alive, a broken alive thing. I am a human being stirring the tea in my chipped cup the color of some kind of river, some kind of serene sea, green-blue and broken-and-glued because it is the cup I love the best. I love to love things. I love to love all the broken things because all people are broken in this way or that, but no one wants to let anyone else in on our shared secret. But there is another secret, and it's that there is beauty. I look for it. I stir it in my cup and dream of the broken people I dream of saving.

I am broken in the heart, in the soul, in the parts that stir, that stir at sad things and lovely things and beautiful things, stir like tea in a chipped cup the color of a river smoothing a rock for hundreds upon hundreds of years. All my breaks are beautiful, like that saved rock dangling from a woman's neck as she dreams of her children and the joy she's known.

I have not put myself back together alone. I have been borne on the backs of the beautiful. They were broken, too, but that's why they knew how to carry me.

***the Japanese art of repairing broken pottery
with lacquer dusted with powdered gold***

Afterword

By Sarah B. Mohler

Although I did not know Rin Kelly, I met her within these pages, just as you will do. The stories in this collection span a wide breadth of genres, Rin's wry humor and keen satirical edge can be found in all of them. In her tribute to Rin published in *The Fabulist*, writer Jenny Bitner noted that Rin wrote about the "basic dehumanization of being alive in late capitalism ... inundated with media, marketing and technology as we try to find our own souls."

Stories such as "Kahlo," "Seven Million Minutes in Heaven," and "White is for Complacent" are scathing indictments of the callousness of the health care system. "Newborn" and "The Breaking News of Charlie Que" critique the exploitive and sensationalist nature of the 24-hour news cycle. "Kahlo" and "Wax Works" point to how casually American society denigrates the working class, women, and people of color. And yet, each of Rin's stories is filled with compassion. Characters in her stories, whether named or unnamed, are all "someones" with their own subjectivity, private loneliness, hidden sorrows, and secret dreams, even if these "someones" are gods transformed into sheep and sex dolls who strive for lives of meaning and beauty.

Many of Rin's stories make reference to canonical literary texts. "Wax Works" is a modern retelling of the myth of Icarus from Ovid's *Metamorphoses* (Bk VIII:183-235). The title for "Sorry Scenes in the Bang-Whimper District," a story that catalogs the numerous tragi-comic deaths that occur on a single street corner, plays on the final lines of T.S. Eliot's poem *The Hollow Men*: "This is the way the world ends/Not with a bang but a whimper." "The Breaking News of Charlie Que (after Franz Kafka)" evokes, in Kafka's trademark absurdist style, both the nightmarish reality of Kafka's *Metamorphosis* as well as the persecution of an ordinary man for imaginary crimes in Kafka's *The Trial*. Although "Sheep, *baah, baah, baah*" takes a facetious tone, we recognize the egomaniacal, grudge-loving gods of Homer and Ovid. However, by eschewing Greek and Roman names and giving the gods ordinary ones, like "Bill," "Jenny," and "Dan," and comparing them to a couple divorcing while their friends take sides, Rin humanizes them while elevating the suffering and angst that humans experience as so much larger and weightier than themselves.

In contrast to these stories, "Tricks in the Cereal Aisle" is inspired by '70s commercials for Trix cereal in which the rabbit mascot is often cruelly deprived of partaking in the cereal by kids who shout, "Silly, rabbit. Trix are for kids!" Anyone who was a child in the '70s is familiar with not only these commercials but also the referendums General Mills orchestrated to coincide with the American presidential elections in which children voted on whether the Trix rabbit should be allowed to eat the cereal he promoted (Brun). Rin's story treats the rabbit as a "someone" with a wife and kids and an ambivalence about his cereal mascot role. Regardless of whether her inspiration derives from the literary canon or pop culture, Rin's wry, biting humor shines, whether she is portraying gods who are in favor of "poly-absolute-ly-everything," poor Charlie Que who has his erection made into an infographic on CNN, or angels interested in market research.

The stories in this collection have been grouped by genre: her New Fabulist and Slipstream stories, her tales of speculative fiction, which focus on her keenly observed realism, and a final section of meditative pieces.

Readers might not be as familiar with New Fabulism and Slipstream. The term "New Fabulism" first came into use in 2002, when in his introduction to Vol. 39 (2002) of the literary journal, *Conjunctions*, guest editor Peter Straub called writers who wrote stories that combine or move between recognized genres "New Fabulists." New Fabulism is a term often used interchangeably with "surrealism" or "magical realism," defined by Marina MacKay as "the intrusion of the fantastical, supernatural, or folkloric happenings or phenomena into an otherwise meticulously delineated, realistic world, where they are treated as unremarkable, requiring no comment or explanation" (201). I am purposely using the terms "New Fabulism" and "Slipstream" to characterize Rin's work because both magical realism and surrealism are contested terms that are each strongly associated with an artistic or literary movement situated in a particular cultural and historical context that blurs the lines of literary influence. For surrealism, this association is with the surrealist art movement of the 1920s and '30s (Bowers 11). For magical realism, it is German Expressionist art of the 1920s and 20th century Latin American literature, specifically the work of Jorge Luis Borges and Gabriel Garcia Marquez (8, 16, 15-16). In contrast, the terms New Fabulism and Slipstream are not so much associated with literary movements or cultural contexts as they are terms to describe a set of literary techniques certain writers use to infuse reality with fantastic elements to express something ineffable that could not be expressed any other way (Wolfe 168). The term "Slipstream" emphasizes how these works tend to slide between genres, whereas the term "New Fabulism" emphasizes the stories as parables whose profound conceptual metaphors illuminate contexts beyond the story itself. As Gary K. Wolfe states in *Evaporating Genres*, stories that use these techniques are charged with "grief, loss, nostalgia, and irreconcilable change, but often attain a feeling of wonder, insight, and hope—even transcendence," which is the feeling I most associate with Rin's work (168-169). Rin's fiction exhibits many of the characteristics Wolfe delineates as belonging to this category of genre-bending fiction: metafictional elements that blur the line between fiction and reality, "self-aware and emotionally powerful storyteller voices," a slippage between genres or a blending of markers from different genres, and the fantastic elements functioning as a "hidden dimension" or "subtext" of reality (169-170, 173).

"Wax Works" utilizes the New Fabulist trope of inserting characters from mythology and folktales into domestic reality, thereby charging reality with a sense of the fantastic and extending the context in which the mythology and folktales can comment on, and "Tricks" does the same for inserting an advertising mascot into the domestic space. "Sheep, *baah, baah, baah*" draws on Slipstream's ability to meld low farce with the elevated discourse of mythology, making the story exist in a realm not quite ancient and not entirely contemporary.

"Kahlo" exemplifies New Fabulism at its best. Ostensibly the story of a poor woman of color who undergoes heart surgery and finds that her heart, still pumping, has been reattached outside of her body, not only speaks to the dehumanizing health care system that victimizes her but succeeds in capturing the universal feeling in these anxiety-inducing times, where all of us feel as if our throbbing hearts have been exposed to a world that will not protect them. This story was the first work of Rin's that I read. It was given to me by my colleague Adam Davis, managing editor of the *Green Hills Literary Lantern*, and its powerful effect inspired me to write this piece.

"The Best-Known Unknown People Who Maybe Drew Breath Upon the Planet," also one of my favorites, has a metafictional exuberance that would appeal to readers of George Saunders and Steven Millhauser. The narrator of this story, like Whitman in "Song of Myself," contains multitudes, but in this case the multitudes are personas expressing contradictory opinions in the op-eds that he feels compelled to publish under false names. This story is New Fabulist in the way each of the personas truly takes on a life of its own in the mind of the narrator and in the minds of the readers of the op-eds, such that it is hard to determine who possesses the more vibrant life: the narrator who lives vicariously through each of these personas or the personas themselves. In these fraught and politically divided times, I find extraordinary hope in this story precisely because it depicts a narrator who has the creativity and empathy to inhabit the minds of so many alternate selves. People close to Rin noted that Rin herself resembled Marjorie, the persona the narrator conjures up who "was just magnificent, all spittle and world-wrecking prose ... you'd feel a kind of happy sorrow in your throat by the end of every letter. By the end, she'd always be calling on us to rise and fight and find our oneness again" (13).

"Sorry Scenes in the Bang-Whimper District," in a similar way to "The Best-Known Unknown People Who Maybe Drew Breath Upon the Planet," binds together disparate individuals who all meet their demise on a particular street corner and narrate the circumstances of their death to the reader. This should not be a hopeful story, and yet, like many New Fabulist stories, it is because anything that emphasizes our shared humanity in the context of our mortality has the ability to make us feel less lonely.

Speculative fiction is fiction that depicts the world as it *could otherwise be*. Thus, it encompasses a whole host of genres, including science fiction, that portray new realities derived from scientific innovation; dystopia, which portrays societal structures or governments that debase human beings and deprive them of their innate rights; and eco-fiction, in which humanity's connection and dependence on nature is the focus on the narrative. "The Breaking News of Charlie Que," while evoking the absurdism of Kafka, also paints for us a dystopian, slightly futuristic world where each of us could be on 24-hour surveillance by the media. "Sentient," which portrays the inner life and yearnings of a sex doll, could easily be read alongside Jeanette Winterson's *Frankissstein* (2019) and Kazuo Ishiguro's *Klara and the Sun* (2021) as a continued exploration of AIs created to be tools and substitutes for human companionship, who develop not only sentience, but self-awareness, and a desire for agency.

Likewise, "Upper Management, or GodCo., LLC" pits one lonely but self-sufficient woman, Priya Argawal, against the angel Raphael, who promises to end suffering by giving humanity "de-lonesoming" AI devices at the mere cost of privacy, self-pride, and participation in a market survey. Trenchant and funny, this story feels all too close to reality after *The Washington Post* broke a story in 2022 that Google engineer Blake Lemoine believed the company's Language Model for Dialogue Applications (LaMDA) chatbot had become sentient (Tiku), raising concerns that even if the chatbot was not sentient, it had passed the Turing test and convinced a high-level researcher that it was. The fact that, in this story, the device is not an earthly invention but the product of a divine corporation suggests that this story could be in dialogue with Dostoevsky's tale of "The Grand Inquisitor" in *The Brothers Karamazov*, in which the church replaces the free will to accept the salvation that Christ offers with the devil's temptation of salvation through the satiation of physical and emotional needs.

This is not the only story that seems to be in conversation with the works of Dostoevsky. In Dostoevsky's *Crime and Punishment*, Svidrigailov wonders if eternity is simply a banal and rather loathsome "bathhouse, covered with soot, with spiders in all the corners," while Rin's narrator in "Seven Million Minutes in Heaven," poses the question, "What if death was just this closet?" while participating in a sensory deprivation experiment that may have killed her or simply warped her perception enough to cast doubt on whether or not she feels alive (304). In contrast to Dostoevsky's Svidrigailov, Rin's narrator finds the closet and the prospect of death peaceful if it weren't for the fear of missing out on the chance to optimize one's life and dull oneself with mindless entertainment: "What good was just being? I could be improving my Scrabble scores right now, but instead I'm dead" (35).

"A Letter from Lakeside" is a biting eco-fictional satire in the form of a complaint letter from a man railing against a liberal government—a man, we later find out, who is destroying the levies that keep his community from flooding. It is all the more devastating when read in the context of flooding, exacerbated by climate change, that has occurred throughout the Midwest, along the coasts, and in Pakistan.

The stories in the third section, *Meditations and Benedictions*, are all set in the real world, but each demonstrates the way certain events or moments in our lives can estrange us from others, from ourselves, and even our grasp on reality. In her 2015 article published in *Salon*, "Do Media Vultures Perpetuate Mass Shootings?" Rin deplores "the mediatization" of trauma and excoriates the way the news media descends upon a town, "thieves its grief and overlays false narratives atop the real," producing "augmented, ongoing pain" and "long-term effects of speculation and copycat-baiting, of simplification and assumption and shallow debate." "Newborn" portrays the experiences of a student who escapes a school shooting and runs, and keeps running, until she dives into a river dyed red to celebrate Christmas, giving her a symbolically bloody rebirth as captured in the photographs of a ravenous news media. In this story, Rin is deeply critical of the exploitive media coverage of school shootings. Her point of view is shaped by first-hand experience, as she and her sister are the daughters and nieces of teachers who survived Columbine. The cruel reality is that both "Newborn" and Rin's 2015 article in *Salon* are as deeply and agonizingly relevant to the coverage of Uvalde in 2022 as they were when Rin first wrote them.

"White is Complacent" depicts two estranged friends, one an addict and one a cop, who are driven apart by their alternate life experiences. "Scattered" portrays the dissolution of a relationship of a couple who fail to complete the jigsaw puzzle they embark on. The uncompleted puzzle becomes a symbol for their inability to discover how their lives should mesh. Rin communicates the tension in the relationship in keenly observed details such as, "She fretted a piece of sky and smeared the fine cardboard dust it left behind onto her jeans. He was pecking border pieces, willfully hearing the rustle and not her reluctance" (94).

"The Bentweed Boys," about children stealing flowers from a grave to give to their mothers, portrays how an offering to the dead serves to beautify the lives of the living, demonstrating how love keeps giving. "Broken Things," dedicated to Brian and Melinda Wilson, is as much about the transmutation of a soul caught in a stone as it is sanded, polished, and eventually set in a woman's necklace, as it is about the woman who wears the necklace, and the chipped teacup she drinks from—all three connected, all three broken, all three beautiful things precisely because they have been broken. Like me, you may read this story and be forever changed, never again raising a teacup or mug to your lips without thinking of beauty in brokenness.

Some lives are long; others are short. The length of a life cannot measure its impact. Rin's life was short, but she continues to be cherished by family and friends. The Writers Grotto Scholarship, established in her honor in 2021, has already supported the creative endeavors of several emerging writers of New Fabulist, Slipstream, and speculative fiction. Her collected short stories, which you hold in your hands, and her novel, *The Bright and Holo Sky*, being readied for publication, will continue to find and touch the lives of readers. Read these stories with bittersweetness and "a happy kind of sorrow."

Works Cited:

Bitner, Jenny. "Remembering Rin Kelly." *The Fabulist*. 26 March 2021. https://fabulistmagazine.com/remembering-rin-kelly/ Accessed 6 Oct. 2022.

Bowers, Maggie Ann. *Magical Realism*. Routledge, 2004.

Brun, Natasha. "Celebrating 60 Years of the Trix Rabbit." General Mills. 12 Aug. 2019. https://www.generalmills.com/news/stories/celebrating-60-years-of-the-trix-rabbit Accessed 6 Oct. 2022.

Dostoevsky, Fyodor. *The Brothers Karamazov*. Translated by Richard Pevear and Larissa Volokhonsky. Picador, 2021.

Dostoevsky, Fyodor. *Crime and Punishment*. Translated by Richard Pevear and Larissa Volokhonsky. Vintage, 2021.

Eliot, T.S. *Complete Poems and Plays*. Faber and Faber, 2004.

Kafka, Franz. *Metamorphosis*. Translated by Susan Bernofsky. W. W. Norton & Company, 2014.

Kafka, Franz. *The Trial*. Translated by Idris Parry. Penguin UK, 2015.

Kelly, Rin. "Do Media Vultures Perpetuate Mass Shootings?" *Salon*. 29 Dec. 2012. https://www.salon.com/2012/12/29/do_media_vultures_perpetuate_mass_shootings/
Accessed 6 Oct. 2022.

Ishiguro, Kazuo. *Klara and the Sun*. Knopf, 2021.

MacKay, Marina. *The Cambridge Introduction to the Novel*. Cambridge University Press, 2011.

Millhauser, Steven. *We Others: New & Selected Stories*. Knopf, 2011.

Ovid. *Metamorphoses*. Translated by A. S. Kline. University of Virginia. https://ovid.lib.virginia.edu/trans/Metamorph8.htm
Accessed 6 Oct. 2022.

Oziewicz, Marek. "Speculative Fiction." *Oxford Research Encyclopedias*. Oxford University Press, 29 March 2017. https://doi.org/10.1093/acrefore/9780190201098.013.78 Accessed 6 Oct. 2022.

Saunders, George. *Liberation Day*. Random House, 2022.

Straub, Peter. *Conjunctions*, vol. 39, 2002.

Tiku, Nitisha. "The Google Engineer Who Thinks the Company's AI Has Come to Life." *The Washington Post*, 11 June 2022. https://www.washingtonpost.com/technology/2022/06/11/google-ai-lamda-blake-lemoine/
Accessed 6 Oct. 2022.

Turner, Mark. *The Literary Mind: The Origins of Thought and Language*. Oxford University Press, 1996.

Whitman, Walt. "Song of Myself." *Leaves of Grass: The First (1855) Edition*. Penguin, 1961.

Winterson, Jeanette. *Frankissstein*. Grove Press, 2019.

Wolfe, Gary K. *Evaporating Genres: Essays on Fantastic Literature*. Wesleyan University Press, 2011.

**Reading recommendations for those who wish
to write New Fabulism:**

"Announcing the 2022 Rin Kelly Scholarship for Fiction." The Writers Grotto.
https://www.sfgrotto.org/rin-kelly-scholarship/ Accessed 6 Oct. 2022.

Bair, Kristen. "Making Magic: Mastering the Art of Magical Realism." *The
Writer's Digest*. 28 Dec. 2018. https://www.writersdigest.com/write-
better-fiction/making-magic-mastering-the-art-of-magical-realism
Accessed 6 Oct. 2022.

Balkun, Stacey. "Using Fabulist Elements to Write the Difficult." 5 April 2016.
https://mockingheartreview.com/2016/04/05/using-fabulist-elements-
to-write-the-difficult/
Accessed 6 Oct. 2022.

Bensko, Tantra. "Write Magical Realism the Right Way." *The Writing Coopera-
tive*. 7 Oct. 2019. https://writingcooperative.com/how-to-write-magical-
realism-c5f19c7763ea
Accessed 6 Oct. 2022.

Haggard, Kit. "How Queer Fabulism Came to Dominate Contemporary Wom-
en's Writing." 8 Aug. 2018. https://theoutline.com/post/5751/fabulism-
fiction-carmen-maria-machado-daisy-johnson-melissa-broder?zd
=1&zi=iqp7j3ka
Accessed 6 Oct. 2022.

"How to Write Magical Realism: 4 Tips for Writing Great Magical Realism."
MasterClass. 23 Aug. 2021. https://www.masterclass.com/articles/how-
to-write-magical-realism#what-is-the-history-of-magical-realism
Accessed 6 Oct. 2022.

Smith, Jack. "Writing Magical Realism: The Ultimate Guide." *The Writer*.
2 March 2022. https://www.writermag.com/improve-your-writing/
fiction/writing-magical-realism/
Accessed 6 Oct. 2022.

Sparks, Amber. "New Genres: Domestic Fabulism or Kansas with a Difference."
Electric Lit. 26 June 2014. https://electricliterature.com/new-genres-
domestic-fabulism-or-kansas-with-a-difference/
Accessed 6 Oct. 2022.

Sarah B. Mohler is an associate professor of English at Truman State University in Kirkville, Missouri, where she also directs the English master's program. She earned her doctorate in Slavic Studies from Princeton University. Her seminars and research focus on Slavic and South Asian literature and film, children's literature, cognitive literary theory, and emerging literary genres, such as New Fabulism and Fake Lit.

Acknowledgments

"Wax Works" was first published in *The Fabulist*. 26 March 2021. The story was shortlisted for a Pushcart Prize. The illustration is by Adam Myers.

"Kahlo" appeared in *The Green Hills Literary Lantern*, Truman State University, Summer, 2022. The illustration, *The Two Fridas*, is by the artist Frida Kahlo, 1939.

"The Best-Known Unknown People Who Maybe Drew Breath Upon the Planet" was published in *The Kenyon Review*, Ohio University, Spring 2015.

"Upper Management, or GodCo., LLC" was chosen by *No Contact*, Columbia University, for the January 2022 issue.

"Seven Million Minutes in Heaven" appeared in *Hobart Pulp*, January 2022. The illustration accompanying the story is by artist Mateo Torre-Bliss.

"The Breaking News of Charlie Que" first appeared in *Penumbric Speculative Fiction Magazine*, October 2021. It was selected for *The Best of Penumbric Anthology*, vol. v. June 2k21 April 2k22.

"Curated" was published in *The Courtship of Winds*, January 2022.

"The Bentweed Boys" appeared in *Steam Ticket, A Third Coast Review, Volume 25, Spring 2022*, University of Wisconsin-LaCrosse, and was reprinted in *DASH Literary Journal, Volume 15*, California State University, Fullerton, and is a Pushcart Prize nominee. The illustration is by British artist Ben East.

"Newborn ~on school shootings" was read at the third annual *Bang, Bang, Gun Amok*, New York City, December 2019. The photo is by retired Columbine art teacher Barb Gal.

"Graceland and Greenland and Disneyland" won first prize out of 500 entries from the Tattered Cover and appeared in *Contemporary Magazine*, The Sunday Denver Post, June 23, 1991.

"White is for Complacent" was published in *Panhandler Magazine*, University of West Florida, Spring 2022.

"Kintsugi – Broken Things" was dedicated to Brian and Melinda Wilson. The kintsugi photo is by Carrie Kelly, John Samson and Judy Reese.

Additional Artwork:

Rin Reimagined is by British artist Ben East, 2014.

Nothing Ever Belongs is by artist Dusty Neu, 2007.

My Grief is the Grief of Birds (inspired by the poem, *Gifts*, by Shu Ting and constructed following the Columbine tragedy) and *No Exit* are by artist/photographer Rin Kelly.

The author photo of Rin Kelly is by Tony Bar.

In Gratitude

For assisting us with compiling this collection, we wish to thank Josh Wilson, Rachel Chalmers, Jenny Bitner, Kimberly Bliss, Susan Peters, John Samson and Jerry Wright. We also appreciate all of the literary magazine editors who saw Rin's gift.

A special shout-out to our illustrators Ben East, Barbara Gal, Mateo Torre-Bliss and Dusty Neu.

We also wish to thank Alex Kale, Ronaldo Alves, Erin Larson, and the Atmosphere Press team.

We are grateful for the crucial contribution of Professor Sarah Mohler for her invaluable elucidation of the contemporary styles in Rin's work. Her description of The New Fabulism, Slipstream and Speculative Fiction brought us new insights into the stories and enhances the collection.

Lastly, we wish to acknowledge the love and support of the Bar family in this presentation of Rin Kelly's legacy and particularly Tony Bar for making this legacy possible.

- The editors **Carrie Kelly**, **Judy Reese** and **Carol Samson**

About the Author

RIN KELLY was a collector of oddments, a critic of culture, a poet. She translated for us, helped us to see what we are. A reader, a lover of words, she graduated from the New School in New York City and earned an M.A. from Columbia University's Toni Stabile School of Journalism. Rin was the life partner of Anthony Bar. They lived in Alameda, California, where she became an investigative journalist, photographer, and fiction writer. She worked as a cultural contributor and film editor at the music publication *L.A. Record*, and as a freelance journalist, publishing articles in *Salon* magazine and in newspapers in New York, Washington, D.C., and the Bay Area. She interviewed the drummer of Talking Heads, traveled on tour buses with drag queens, made friends with animal rescue groups, and fostered small dogs and kittens. And, too, Rin continually wrote fiction and worked on her soon-to-be released novel.

This collection contains stories published in many literary journals and magazines, including *The Kenyon Review* and *The Fabulist*. Two of these stories are recent Pushcart Prize nominees, one shortlisted for the Prize. The collection, published posthumously, is Rin's legacy to us. Mostly speculative fiction, the stories show her to be a writer much like the letter writer she describes in one of her stories: a writer with "spittle," one capable of "world-wrecking prose," yet one who demonstrates "so much dignity and clemency that you'd feel a kind of happy sorrow in your throat by the end." Rin Kelly understood the power of words. She was a quick questioner, a witness to broken things, a writer who asks us to consider the "matters" of the world—some that will melt us, some that will offer us calla lilies.

Rin knew that, in the end, we all become words, we all become stories. She continues here.

9 7 9 8 8 9 1 3 2 0 4 6 8